Nicky's throat thickened. She swallowed coffee and choked on the hot, black liquid.

Distracted by the outline of Meg's body under her thin T-shirt, she asked, "What do you want to talk about?"

Easing into a relaxed position, she smiled at Nicky. "I don't want to talk."

Nicky's heart hammered erratically. She gripped her coffee cup with whitened fingers. She had known this moment was coming; she just hadn't known when or what she would do when it did. Noticing Meg's tongue dart over her lips, she licked her own.

Meg reached for Nicky's hand. "Come on." When Nicky shook her head, she said, "Please."

Sunlight covered the quilt on the bed, the braided rug on the wood floor. The whites, reds, greens, blues and browns looked bright and clean. Nicky felt as if she were in a dream. She told herself it wasn't too late to say no, but something inside her wanted to know what Meg would be like in bed. She remembered the preview.

About the Author

Jackie Calhoun is the author of *Lifestyles, Second Chance, Sticks and Stones,* and *Friends and Lovers* — all published by Naiad Press. She recently finished her sixth novel, *Accidental Changes* (1995) and has started work on her seventh. She has stories in two anthologies, *The Erotic Naiad* and *The Romantic Naiad.* She lives in Wisconsin with her partner.

TRIPLE EXPOSURE

BY JACKIE CALHOUN

THE NAIAD PRESS, INC.
1994

Printed in the United States of America on acid-free paper
First Edition

Edited by Christine Cassidy
Cover design by Bonnie Liss (Phoenix Graphics)
Typeset by Sandi Stancil

Library of Congress Cataloging-in-Publication Data

Calhoun, Jackie.
Triple exposure / Jackie Calhoun.
p. cm.
ISBN 1-56280-067-1
1. Lesbians—Middle West—Fiction. I. Title.
PS3553.A3985T74 1994
813′.54—dc20 94-16240
CIP

To my longtime Indiana friend,
Kay,
who introduced me to the world of horses,
and to my daughters,
who shared it with me,
and to Dick,
a reluctant participant.

Although some of the locations in this book may resemble actual places, the characters and story are fiction.

I

The wind, blowing through the truck windows, offered Nicky no relief from the heat. Instead, it piled clouds into outlandish shapes and chased them across the sky, causing a few drops of rain to spatter against the dusty windshield. Nicky ran slender fingers through sweat-blackened hair plastered to her neck as the tires of the Ford F250 strummed across warning strips. Glancing at the gas gauge, she turned into the station at Wisconsin state highways 10 and 110.

She had risen at dawn on this first Sunday in

June and driven west in search of sandhill cranes to photograph. Instead of the cranes, which remained elusive, she had filmed lilac bushes growing in profusion around abandoned buildings and fields of wild mustard cut through by a trout stream.

As she shoved the nozzle into the gas tank, her attention was drawn to the other side of the concrete island of pumps where a woman kicked at the rear tire of an aging Volkswagen Rabbit.

"It's too goddamn hot for this," the woman quietly cursed.

Admiring ash-blonde curls falling toward broad shoulders and long tan legs covered only by shorts, Nicky rested a hand against the super cab and asked hesitantly, "Something wrong?"

The woman wrenched around, showing Nicky a face resembling the thunderclouds overhead — dark gray eyes, frowning brows, a pouting sensual mouth. Then she cleared away the anger with a sheepish smile. "Sorry, but it won't start. I think the battery's really dead this time, and now this tire's going flat." She pointed a toe at the offending tire she had just kicked. "Can you help me push it out of the way?"

"Why don't you have someone here put in a new battery?"

"No one does service work at these convenience centers, but there's a place just over the bridge in Fremont where they do." The woman opened the driver's door, leaned into the frame with one hand on the steering wheel, and looked expectantly at Nicky.

After they pushed the Rabbit to the edge of the blacktop next to a field of young corn, Nicky straightened and brushed her hands together, then extended one. "Nicky Hennessey," she said.

"You look like an Irishwoman — dark hair, blue eyes. I'm Meg Klein." The woman grinned, showing off deep dimples and white teeth.

"Can I give you a lift?"

"Yeah, sure. That service station across the river."

Nicky nodded and gestured toward the building. "Let me pay for the gas and get something to drink. Okay?"

"I have to pay, too," Meg remarked with a wry twist to her mouth.

When they climbed into the Ford, Nicky said, "Have you had breakfast?" The ice-cold Pepsi she had just guzzled hadn't quenched her thirst.

"Nope, but I'm ready for lunch."

"Want to catch a bite with me while they work on your car? I think there's a restaurant next to the station."

"Sounds like a good idea."

While Meg rode with the wrecker back to get her car, Nicky waited with the truck door open, her thighs sticking to the vinyl seat. The brief shower had stopped. She glanced at blue sky behind torn clouds and thought how hot it would be if the sun came out.

The air-conditioned restaurant set her shivering. Sliding into a booth cushioned with red vinyl seats, Nicky pressed her bare arms close to her body — searching for some of the warmth she had just been complaining about. Hearing rain, she noticed water streaming down the windows, saw steam rising from the pavement.

Meg's gaze followed Nicky's. "Looks like we got inside just in time. Am I keeping you from wherever you're going?"

"Home." Nicky smiled briefly. Home on the range she couldn't afford.

"And where's that?"

"I've got a little place in the country near the Fox Cities." It had been listed in the weekly *Trader's Guide* as a "farmette for the handyman." In actuality, it was an old house with dilapidated outbuildings on a few acres of weeds. The wiring had been bare in places, the floors grimy, the walls in need of paint. The barn had been and still was falling down. Beth had helped her with the necessary improvements, perhaps to appease Nicky for not leaving her husband, Mark. That had been two years ago.

Meg returned the smile. "I live in town. I work at Fox Cities Med Center as a medical technician. I've been looking for another place to keep my horse."

Nicky watched Meg's gray eyes brighten, the dimples deepen, and she wanted to capture the expressive face on film. "I'm a photographer. I work at the Art Barn to pay the bills, though." Here it was June fifth and she hadn't paid the mortgage. She never should have bought the place expecting Beth to move in.

Meg eyed her speculatively. "Would you consider boarding a horse? "

Caught by surprise, Nicky stammered, "I don't know. There is a barn. It's not in the best of shape, but I suppose it could be used. And the pasture's fenced in."

"I'd pay, of course," Meg said excitedly, "and I can help with repairs."

Grinning, Nicky held up a hand against Meg's enthusiasm. "Not so fast. I don't know anything about horses." She thought for a moment. "Why don't you come see the place first, then we'll talk seriously if you still want to." Perhaps taking in this horse would bring in some easy money. She had been considering a roommate to help defray costs. A horse wouldn't cramp her style, wouldn't impose on her independence, would make no demands on her time.

"All right," Meg agreed. "I'll come out tomorrow after work, if that's okay." She smiled broadly. "Now I'm glad my car broke down."

Nicky turned into her long driveway. It was early afternoon. The rain had stopped shortly after she left the restaurant. Bouncing through puddles, the truck sent muddy water flying toward the small, barking dog running alongside. For the first time in months she really noticed the rundown barn.

The dog had appeared a couple weeks ago and so far had refused to leave. She had asked around at nearby houses and farms but no one had claimed him. He was cute, she had to admit. His black curling hair led her to believe that he carried poodle genes mixed with maybe cocker or schnauzer. His tail curved high over his back and his eyes lay hidden behind the tangle of hair.

Slamming the truck door, she warned him, "Don't you dare jump on me." She saw a tiny glimmer of teeth before he followed her to the barn — so close on her heels, he sometimes touched her leg with his nose.

She pushed open the sagging, resisting door and stepped inside. Dust rose from leftover moldering hay and straw and she sneezed. Stanchions for the former occupants filled the lower level. She could almost hear the lowing of cattle as she stood there on the concrete floor, the cement walls surrounding her, and the low-beamed ceiling overhead. To her right had been the milk room, the telltale vats still in place. Next to it was an empty room, to store grain maybe. The floor above, a large, open space with slippery footing, had once housed equipment. It was enclosed by boards with gaps between them that let in wind and rain, and accessed by huge tracked doors that flapped in the weather and were reached from a grassy incline. Not a safe place for a horse. The hay mow occupied the third floor. There were shuttered windows front and back that could be reached by hay elevators. A trap door in the floor and a ladder provided regular entry.

Thinking that perhaps Meg would change her mind upon seeing what she was getting for her money, Nicky steeled herself against unexpected disappointment. She had thought she would, instead, feel relief.

The old house greeted her with blank windows. Fancying she could still smell the years of neglect, she threw open all the first-floor windows that weren't painted shut. Then she sat on the front porch and silently weighed the pros and cons of boarding a horse. She tried to ignore the dog, who stretched out on the stoop, occasionally scratching frantically at his matted coat.

"I don't want to love another dog," she said to him, remembering her last dog with regret and a touch of guilt. She had let him run free only to end up under the wheels of a speeding car.

The following evening after work, she and Meg

stood in what Nicky assumed had been the feed room of the barn, next to the milk room, a wide door opening it to the outside. The night before she had asked Dan, the neighboring farmer, if he would help with the fencing.

"So, this is it." Nicky smiled apologetically. "We could put a fence out here to connect with the pasture fence. My neighbor, Dan, said he'd dig the postholes."

"Yeah, it might work," Meg agreed, her lower lip caught between her teeth. She stooped to pat the dog who sniffed suspiciously at her hand.

Nicky watched her carefully, getting those vibes she had gotten at their first meeting. Without knowing why, she was certain that Meg was gay and just as sure that Meg knew she was too — the unspoken communication between two people with the same sexual orientation.

"It's not much," she apologized with a wave of her arm for what she had to offer — the decrepit condition of the barn and existing fences. "What do you think?" she continued, her heartbeat picking up speed at the thought of Meg possibly changing her mind. And not just because she needed the money, which she did, but also because it would be nice to have someone around on a regular basis.

Meg looked at her. "How much?"

Taken aback because she hadn't thought about what she should charge, she said, "I don't know. What sounds fair?"

"Well, I'll pay for his feed and stuff like the blacksmith and veterinarian, of course, and I'll take care of him. I can probably swing a hundred a month." Meg's gray eyes smiled.

Jubilant, Nicky let a slow, pleased smile stretch across her face. A hundred and she didn't have to do diddly-squat! Except make things ready, of course. "What's his name? What does he look like?"

"I assume that means yes?" Meg questioned and Nicky nodded. "Brittle's his name, Skippy's Peanut Brittle. He's sorrel with three white socks and a strip on his face." Meg looked momentarily doleful. "He's kind and friendly and a wonderful ride, but he costs an arm and a leg to keep."

"Dan said he could dig the postholes Saturday." She watched Meg once more run a hand over the smelly little dog. Embarrassed by the animal's filthy coat, she explained, "He's not mine. He showed up here one day, and he won't leave."

"We've got a cat," Meg said, getting into her Rabbit. "I'll be here bright and early Saturday. Thanks, Nicky." She departed in a cloud of dust.

Nicky watched her leave with misgivings. The arrangement seemed too easily made. There had to be a catch.

The next day after work she drove to the lumberyard to pick up fencing and posts. Dan had advised woven fence over barbed wire. When she paid the clerk, it occurred to her that Brittle was costing her money even before she realized a profit on him. Oh well, she silently reasoned, to make money you usually have to spend some.

Saturday dawned hot and clear. Mildly excited, Nicky stepped outside and stretched. She checked the fence post stakes, then looked up the road toward Dan's place. He had promised to come over after milking.

Meg's arrival stirred up another dust bath. They'd had no rain since their meeting nearly a week ago. Meg slammed the door of the Rabbit and strode toward Nicky. She wore jeans and a T-shirt and tennis shoes.

Meg's breasts were bouncing slightly, her tanned face framed by sun-bleached curls, her gray eyes large and shining. Nicky steeled herself to resist any attraction.

"Am I early enough?"

"How about some coffee?"

Sun streamed through the windows of the large kitchen, nourishing Nicky's many plants hanging from the ceiling. Even though the joy had gone out of the place for her without Beth, the walls and linoleum looked bright and warm in the light and the white-painted cabinets appeared clean and appealing, as did the old countertops.

"Nice," Meg said, looking around the room.

"It's just an old farmhouse," Nicky said deprecatingly, knowing its many shortcomings, especially the lack of storage and workspace. Once, as a proud owner, she might have pointed out the pantry and commented on the quiet nights. Now she couldn't summon the enthusiasm.

"I love old houses."

Nicky groaned under her breath. She wasn't interested in meeting another woman who might break her heart with unkept promises. Over the barking of the dog she heard the sounds of a tractor.

“That dog thinks he owns the place,” she grunted. Handing Meg her cup of coffee, she went for the door. “Dan’s here.”

Over six feet tall and husky with dark, unruly hair and brown eyes set in a ruddy face, Dan was weathered from his many hours outside. Nicky had at first guessed him to be about her own age, thirty-five, and was surprised to learn that he was six years younger.

It took less than half an hour to dig the holes. Although Nicky protested that she and Meg could finish off, Dan helped drop the posts into position, fill the holes, and stretch the fencing. “I owe you,” she said to him when the new fence met the old.

“No, you don’t. You let me use this pasture last summer.”

“True,” she said. He had fixed fence, replaced posts.

When Dan left, she and Meg walked the perimeter of the pasture. Having chased the tractor off the property, the little dog bounded ahead of them through new grass already up to his belly. They came to the creek and Nicky was considering how to cross it.

“I won’t even have to water Brittle,” Meg exclaimed, removing her tennis shoes and sticking a foot into the burbling, dark water. “Cold, icy,” she said, quickly crossing.

Nicky found herself staring at the patches of sweat between and under Meg’s breasts and with an effort glanced away from the damp spots.

When they returned to the barn, Meg said she had to go see to the horse. “I have to rent a truck and trailer if I'm going to bring him here tomorrow." That was the time frame they had agreed to.

"I could help. We could use my truck," Nicky suggested without thought.

"Hey, that would be great," Meg said, standing with her weight on one leg — one hand on the car door, the other on her hip.

The next morning started out cloudy and sticky, threatening rain. Nicky met Meg at the rental store where they picked up the horse trailer. From there they drove to the barn where Meg had been boarding her horse. When Nicky parked in front of the fancy stable, she realized what a comedown it must be to both Meg and the horse to have to move to her place.

She followed Meg into the stable to get Brittle, who nickered softly from behind the bars of his stall. Taking a halter from a hook next to the stall door, Meg slid the door open and slipped the halter over the large head.

The size of the animal daunted Nicky. She hadn't expected him to be so big, nearly sixteen hands, according to Meg. Nicky was glad she wouldn't be the one providing care and handling. All she had to do was look at him from the other side of a fence.

"Would you hold him? I have to get his stuff." Meg thrust the lead rope at her.

She quailed inside. "I don't know how." But Meg only smiled absently and walked away. Brittle stared at Nicky with large, sorrowful, brown eyes. He took a dump on the spotless aisle floor. Nicky moved a few steps away from the pile, and he followed her.

A horse nickered from a nearby stall and Brittle tossed his head a little and answered. He moved sideways and Nicky, her heart hammering a fast tattoo against her ribs, hung onto the lead rope as if the horse were plotting to escape. Where the hell was Meg?

Fifteen minutes passed before Meg returned and led the horse outside. Brittle clambered into the trailer as if walking into a dark, narrow box were commonplace for him. Did he do whatever was asked of him? Nicky wondered. All Meg had done was point him toward the open door and cluck a couple times, then close the tailgate behind him and fasten his head through the little window up front.

Later, they stood by the fence as the sorrel horse investigated his new surroundings. His legs buckled under him and he rolled outside the barn, then struggled upright and, emitting a squeal punctuated by a string of startlingly loud farts, galloped across the pasture. Clumps of sod flew from his hooves. Barking, the little dog took a few running steps after him. Then, as if thinking better of it, he stopped and looked from Nicky to Meg and back again.

"Smart dog," Meg said. "He could get his face kicked in. Doesn't he have a name?"

Nicky shook her head. To give him a name would be to acknowledge his presence as possibly permanent. Pretending indifference to Brittle's alarming behavior, she turned away from the fence.

"Look," Meg said, toeing the ground. "I wonder if you could put some grain in that ground feeder for him tonight." They had unloaded several bags of feed and stored them in the old milk room. “I have to go somewhere. Something I can’t beg out of.”

Nicky hesitated, words of protest crowding her thoughts, then said nothing. After all, it was only one night, and she had Meg’s first check for one hundred dollars.

That evening she poured the feed into the tub and hurried out of the enclosure as the horse raced from the pasture toward her. He seemed to know that dinner was served. “Hey,” she said when Brittle first nosed the tub, then pawed it, spilling the grain onto the ground.

Looking up at the sound of a vehicle, half expecting it to be Meg again, she recognized Beth’s car, a black Ford Probe. Beth emerged from the driver’s seat looking as sleek as the car. Her thick, light brown hair was piled on top of her head. She wore cotton slacks, a short-sleeved cotton sweater and loafers. She bent to touch the dog, who had rushed to greet her.

“Give him a name yet?”

“He’s not staying. I’m sure he already has a name — we just don’t know what it is.”

“That’s what you think. He’s here for the duration. How about calling him Scrappy?”

Ignoring the suggestion, Nicky said, “Come see my new roomie.”

“Where did he come from?” Beth exclaimed upon seeing Brittle. “Isn’t he elegant?”

“He doesn’t belong to me.” Nicky told her about the events that had led the horse to her barn.

“He’s a gelding, probably a Quarter Horse. Is he registered?”

"Yes. How do you know those things?" Nicky was impressed.

While Brittle crunched grain between strong yellow teeth, Beth leaned over and pointed. "He's been cut, so he can't become a daddy. And he looks like a Quarter Horse. The American Quarter Horse Association is the world's fastest growing horse breed registry and the largest," she said knowingly.

"No kidding." Nicky grinned, glad to see her. "Will you stay for supper?"

"Love to. I tried to call you all day."

"I've been outside. Let's go throw some food together." Still dressed in sweat-stained shorts and T-shirt, she put an arm around Beth and led her toward the house.

She and Beth had attended high school together, had been lovers while roommates at the University of Wisconsin-Madison. Heartbroken when Beth exhibited signs of heterosexuality, Nicky nevertheless agreed to be the maid of honor at her wedding. Shortly thereafter, Nicky left the university without graduating and returned to the Fox Cities, and Beth forged ahead toward her law degree. It seemed impossible that fifteen years had passed.

"Where's your handsome young son?"

"At home with his dad." Beth paused outside the back door. The dog panted between them. "I missed you."

"Me too." Nicky pushed the door inward, placing a restraining foot against the dog's chest as he tried to squeeze inside with them. "How d'you know so much about horses, Ms. Forrester?"

"I have a client who shows Quarter Horses. I've ridden some of their stock."

"Really?" Nicky felt desire stir. She admired Beth, who always seemed to know what she wanted out of life and how to get it.

Despite the idle conversation, she knew why Beth was there — and alone. Their love affair had resumed a year after Matt's birth, when Beth and Mark moved to the Fox Cities to join his father's law practice.

Nicky hadn't been able to resist saying, "You never should have married, you know."

To which Beth had replied, "I never would have had Matt otherwise."

Looking into Beth's clear, hazel eyes, Nicky thought ruefully that Beth still had Mark and Matt and Nicky. She understood why Beth loved Matt so much. At ten years of age, he endeared himself to Nicky too with his gentle, friendly ways. On the other hand, she hardly knew Mark. She was fairly certain, though, that he knew nothing of Beth's affair with her.

As the bedroom darkened around them later, Nicky murmured into Beth's slender neck, "You smell wonderful, you taste wonderful, you look wonderful."

Beth burbled soft laughter. "So do you, sweetie."

"But I wish things were different." Nicky sighed deeply, kissing the space between Beth's winged collarbone. They lay hot and languid from lovemaking in Nicky's double bed. "I want you to stay the night." She breathed the request into Beth's rosy lips as she ran a warm, persuasive hand over her slippery, smooth skin.

Beth struggled to a sitting position. "I love you, Nicky, but I have to get back."

Nicky propped herself on an elbow, the sheet

falling off her breasts. "Matthew would love it here, especially with a horse."

Beth paused while gathering her clothes to glance at Nicky. Her voice softened. "Look at you. You have the nicest breasts." Then, "The kid loves Little League baseball too. He's a city boy. Want to take a shower?"

Afterwards, they dried each other and dressed and started for the door.

Beth's eyes smiled into Nicky's. "Listen, this was a nice evening. Let's don't spoil it with demands."

Nicky experienced a brief moment of despair. Beth never made any demands. She seemed happy with things as they were. But she only said, "I love you, Beth. Give my love to Matthew."

"I will, sweetie. Look who's here waiting for us — Scrappy. There's nothing as devoted as a dog. You really ought to clean him up."

They passed the sweet-smelling honeysuckle bush on their way to Beth's Probe, and Nicky watched the car swallowed up by distance and the night. She said to the dog, "Scrappy, huh? It fits." Suddenly lonely, she went over to the new fence but couldn't see even a shadow of Brittle in the pasture.

II

The next morning, parked behind the Art Barn, Nicky let herself in the rear door. The old wood floors creaked under her tennis shoes as she made her way past paintings and prints, sculptures and pottery, to the square counter at the center of the building. Fans hung from the high ceilings, lazily stirring the air.

Margo, her bleached blonde hair stacked untidily on top of her head, looked up over half-glasses and welcomed Nicky with a smile. She wore a smock and long skirt over her large frame. "I just sold one of your photographs."

"Really? Which one?"

"*Spring.*" Margo's prominent pale, blue eyes met Nicky's in a moment of pleased acknowledgment. By offering Nicky a job at the Art Barn, Margo had given her an opportunity to show and sell her work. Nicky earned her paycheck by framing pictures for customers and tending the store in Margo's absence.

Nicky flushed. She disliked naming her photos, but Margo insisted, claiming that the titles helped to sell the prints.

"Did you take any pictures this weekend?"

She hadn't and silently wondered why. She mentioned Brittle, thinking he might make a good photography subject.

Burying herself in the back room all morning, Nicky made a valiant attempt to catch up with framing orders. Around noon Margo stuck her head in the door to say she was leaving for a while, could Nicky keep an eye out for customers. When the front door jangled, Nicky reluctantly put aside her work.

"We could run off with some valuable art here," Beth called, one arm around Matthew.

Wiping her hands on her work apron, Nicky smiled, pleased to see the two of them. "If we had anything valuable to run off with. How you doing, Matt? Batting a thousand?"

"Naw," the boy admitted. He was small and skinny with straight brown hair and eyes like his mother's. He readjusted his ball cap and jerked it down over his forehead. "I brought in the winning run yesterday," he said proudly.

"Did you?" Nicky pulled the bill of his cap down even more, covering long-lashed, hazel eyes. "Did your mother tell you about Brittle?"

"Yeah." He tipped his head back in order to meet her eyes. "Can I see him?"

"He's a big dude. Maybe if Meg's there, you can ride him. Would you like that?"

Beth, looking cool and lovely in a tailored rayon suit, said, "We can only stay a few minutes. I have to take Matt to practice and get back to the office. Thought we could set something up for Matt to meet the horse Saturday."

"Sounds good. I'll call you soon as I talk to Meg," Nicky said to Beth. Then to Matt, "Take care of that right arm." She winked at him, and he grinned shyly in return.

Meg was grooming Brittle when Nicky arrived home that evening. The horse was tied to a fence post in the small lot just outside the barn. Mosquitoes droned overhead, and the air smelled faintly of citronella. Nicky leaned on the fence to watch. Scrappy left her side to nose the manure piles.

Meg shooed him out of the enclosure. "Dogs sometimes eat manure," she said.

Nicky glanced down. Was he that hungry? "Maybe I should feed him, but then he'd never leave."

"Would you like to ride?"

Nicky laughed. "No, thanks." She watched admiringly as Meg put a pad, a Western saddle and bridle on the horse and mounted him.

"He rides double," Meg said, looking down at her.

Nicky shook her head emphatically and followed the fence so that she could keep them in view. She had never seen a horse, not even in the movies, that didn't toss its head or swish its tail when ridden, that didn't run off on a loose rein. Astonished, she watched Brittle canter across the pasture like a huge rocking horse.

A warm breeze washed over her as the low-lying sun set the western sky aflame and turned puffy clouds pink overhead. A few early lightning bugs flashed on and off in the meadow. Nicky retrieved her camera from the floor of the truck and snapped several shots of horse and rider silhouetted against the colors of the sky.

Before going home Meg joined her for a beer on the screened-in front porch. They could see nothing outside but an occasional firefly. June bugs buzzed and moths shredded velvety wings against the screens in vain attempts to reach the lights.

Nicky got up and switched off the overhead bulb. The blackness of the night sky, relieved by a nearly full moon and countless glittering stars, slowly revealed itself. The June bugs and moths ceased their frantic efforts to get inside. The wind had vanished with the sun, and the night surrounded them with warm, pulsing darkness.

"This is great," Meg said, settling back on the chaise lounge. "I could fall asleep here."

"I often do," Nicky replied. "Have you always had a horse?"

"Nope. Brittle's my first."

"What made you buy him?"

"I didn't. I inherited him." Nicky could feel Meg's eyes on her. "And now I'm hiding him."

A few heartbeats of silence followed this remark.

Just her luck, she thought, the horse must be hot. "Why?"

"I told my roommate, Denise, that I sold him. Why do you think I drive that beat-up car? He eats all my spare cash."

Nicky failed to understand. "But why do you have to tell her anything? It's your money, isn't it?"

"I know that, you know that, even she knows that." Nicky saw the shadow of a fatalistic shrug. "Which reminds me, I'd better be going. She'll be wondering where I am."

Nicky accompanied Meg to her car and stood slapping at mosquitoes while the Rabbit vanished into the satiny night. Hurrying back to the porch, she made a bed out of the chaise lounge and, wrapped in a sheet, stared at the sky until her eyes closed in sleep.

Brittle chased her across the pasture in her dreams that night. She hid behind the few trees, trying to escape his persistent pursuit, and awoke with a pounding heart to the hush before dawn. Forcing herself to stay awake so that she wouldn't return to the dream, she watched shadowy objects solidify as daylight turned the sky a deep blue. The hush ended with the first bird's chirp, followed by the early morning chorus that would not die away until nesting season was over. Some mornings she cursed the symphony of birds that ended her sleep.

Standing barefoot in the bathroom, she stared at her face in the mirror. Freckles brought out by the summer sun marched across her nose and cheeks. Her disheveled black hair stood on end where it was cut short on top and flattened where it curled down the back of her neck. Her dark blue eyes looked gummy with sleep. "Who would want to wake up to you?" she said, wishing that Beth did.

The following Saturday morning, Nicky waited in her kitchen with Beth and Matthew. Matt had just stuffed an entire piece of coffee cake into his mouth, and Nicky couldn't take her eyes off him. Beth was reading the paper. He washed the coffee cake down with milk and wiped his lips with the back of one hand.

Hearing the sound of the Rabbit, Nicky swallowed the dregs of her coffee. "That's Meg. Ready to go?"

The boy grabbed another piece of coffee cake, which he fed to the dog. "Can we take him home, Mom?" he begged.

"He does need a home," Nicky said to Beth.

"He has a home. He's good company for you. We're gone all day," Beth pointed out.

Meg was shaking a bucket of grain near where the new fence met the old. She stood her ground when Brittle, snorting excitement, skidded to a stop a foot from her and buried his nose in the pail. Slipping the halter over his long ears, she led him toward the barn. Matthew hung on the fence, his eyes wide.

"I hear you want to ride," Meg said.

"Maybe," he replied. "Does he like people riding him?"

"I think he does," Meg said, "especially kids. I'll

tell you what. I'll put him on a longe line and you can ride that way."

Matt climbed the fence and jumped down on the other side. "What's a longe line?"

"You'll see."

Feeling Beth's warm shoulder touching her own, Nicky pressed against her. They were the same height — toe-lockers, Nicky often said — around five-foot-four inches. She smiled into Beth's gold-flecked eyes, shaded like her son's by curling dark lashes. "You're gorgeous," she whispered.

"You're full of sweet shit," Beth murmured back.

In the field Meg gave the boy a leg up, then urged the horse to move in large circles around her, his halter fastened to a long nylon lead which she controlled.

Patting Beth's hand reassuringly, Nicky said, "She knows what she's doing." Something she only assumed. And despite her dream, she added, "Anyway, he's harmless."

"Nothing that big is ever harmless."

They watched as Matt bounced precariously, clutching the saddle horn. Meg called instructions to him, "Straighten your back, sit deep, get your heels down, move with the horse," and then encouragement, "Atta boy."

The sun baked them where they stood. Matt didn't look like he was having a good time, Nicky thought. It pained her to watch him jerk like a loose sack of potatoes. "Want to wade in the creek?" she suggested to Beth.

"How can I? He might fall off."

"Are you planning to catch him?"

Throwing Nicky an annoyed look, Beth snapped, "All right," and strode off through the tall grass.

"Where's the fire?" Nicky asked, hurrying to keep up.

Beth slowed her step. "Sorry."

"What are you doing the rest of the day? Can you stay?"

"This afternoon Matt has a game and tonight we've been invited to dinner. Clients," she added, smiling apologetically.

Nicky struggled to keep the disappointment out of her voice. "When do we get another Saturday together?"

Spreading her arms, palms up, Beth shrugged. "When I can arrange it. It's just real hard. Mark doesn't understand."

They had reached the stream where it turned a corner, undercutting its bank. Nicky sat down and leaned against the trunk of a weeping willow. The dog plopped full length on one side of her, while Beth sat on the other. Beth reached for her hand and Nicky pulled it away, asking, "Why would he?"

"Look, you want me to tell him?"

Giving her a dark look, Nicky said between clenched teeth, "I don't want you to do anything you don't want to do." She thought that was the truth. The little dog licked her face, and for the first time she saw his large adoring eyes peering out from under shaggy black brows. If he hadn't smelled so bad, she might have smiled, might not have held him at arm's length.

"I'll come early tomorrow. Okay?"

"Once a week, is that all the time we're ever

going to have? But I suppose you're getting it in between." Nicky looked away. Her jaw was beginning to ache.

"You sound like Matt when he doesn't get his way," Beth said, leaning forward attempting to make eye contact.

Nicky jumped to her feet. "Let's go back before I say something I shouldn't." She saw Meg leading Brittle toward the barn, Matt still mounted on his back. Scrappy raced toward them.

"Like what?"

"It doesn't matter."

"We'll talk tomorrow. Why don't you ask Meg to do something tonight?"

Nicky snorted a laugh. "You don't care? She's gay, you know." A peculiar look crossed Beth's face. "Taste something bad?"

"Yes. You're threatening me."

"No, I'm not. You'll know when I am."

They had reached the barn and Matthew was running toward them. "Did you see me, Mom? Meg says I'm a natural."

"I'm real proud of you, sweetie. You looked like a cowboy up there. Just needed a hat, didn't he, Nicky?"

"And boots. I was impressed."

"Didn't he do great?" Meg enthused. "I can't believe it was his first time on horseback. With a few lessons he'd be ready to hit the show circuit."

"You want to learn to ride, honey?" Beth asked him.

"Yeah. Can I?"

"Do you teach riding, Meg?"

Now Nicky understood. Brittle was going to pay

for his keep. She grasped her arms, feeling the fire of the sun on her skin, as she listened to Beth and Meg make tentative arrangements for lessons. Then in front of Beth, she asked Meg, "Doing anything tonight?"

"Nope. Denise is out of town visiting her parents." Meg carried the Western saddle into the milk room and stood it on its pommel. "What do you have in mind?"

"Why don't we eat here and then go out?" Nicky suggested. "Let me walk Beth and Matt to their car. Be right back."

"This evening was your idea," she said, looking into the Probe at Beth. It gave her a perverse pleasure. "Bye Matt."

"Hope you have a good time," Beth said.

She watched, enveloped by dust, as the Probe sped out of the driveway.

While Meg finished up with Brittle, Nicky warmed up Ragu, cooked spaghetti and put together tossed salad. When they sat down to eat that evening, she asked Meg about Denise. The overhead fan whirred quietly, keeping the hot air in motion.

"I've been with Denise nearly seven years now, ever since I was twenty-six. She's thirteen years older than I am and thinks we should buy a house." Curling spaghetti around her fork, she frowned. "I know I should tell her I still have Brittle, but these lessons will help pay for his keep." She looked at Nicky as if asking for approval.

Nicky shrugged. "I don't understand, I guess, because I don't think anyone should tell you how to spend your money. Maybe I've been alone too long."

A strand of spaghetti swiped her chin on its way to her mouth. Wiping her face with a napkin, she changed the subject. "What do you want to do tonight?"

"We could go to a movie or get a video."

"Let's go out," Nicky said. "Sometimes I need to get away from here, and tonight is one of those times."

"Anyone you want to talk about?"

"Not really." She was looking for distraction, not soul-searching.

After the movie, they went to the only gay bar in the Valley. "You sure you want to do this?" Nicky asked, noticing Meg's nervousness, her furtive glances.

"Why shouldn't we be here together?" Meg asked defensively, squaring her shoulders. "Want to dance?"

The music reverberated off the walls and ceilings, a relentless pounding beat, making normal conversation impossible. They joined the couples on the dance floor, moving to their own rhythm. An hour passed, then two, while they drank beer, danced, breathed the hot smoky air and shouted to each other and anyone they recognized. The back door was open and often Nicky stepped outside to look at the clear night, to ease the hammering in her ears and to escape from the heat and smoke.

"You coming out tomorrow?" Nicky asked on the drive home.

"Probably. I have to take care of Brittle, and Denise won't be home till late afternoon."

Around ten a.m. Sunday Nicky started watching for Beth's Probe, peering up the road toward town. By one she was pissed, at three-thirty she was furious. Meg arrived early afternoon and left a few minutes before Beth showed up at five. Nicky was in a rage.

"I'm sorry. I just couldn't get away." Beth followed Nicky toward the house. She placed a hand on Nicky's arm, only to have it shaken off.

Opening the screen door, Nicky fell over Scrappy. He let out a yelp that raised goose bumps all over her. "Damn, fucking dog." She slammed the door, shutting him outside.

Beth laughed, covering her mouth with a hand when Nicky shot her a filthy look. "Oops. Sorry, sweetie. You gave him a bath, didn't you?"

"I had lots of time on my hands. I had to do something with it." She had not only given him a scrubbing, noticing his ribby condition, but had also fed him some real dog food she had picked up with the groceries. He had wormed his way into her life. "And I'm not your sweetie. Mark is. He's the one you choose to live with. So what do you want with me?" she asked peevishly, detesting herself for it.

"I love you." Beth took Nicky's arms and forcefully turned her until they faced each other. "I never promised to leave him. I think it would be impossible to work in his dad's firm if I left him for a woman."

"Would he have to know?" she asked, knowing they were repeating old questions and arguments.

"Because of Matthew, he would know. It would come out."

Nicky had pondered these arguments until they bored even her. She told herself not to spoil the evening with futile demands and pointless accusations.

Looking in the grocery bags Beth had set on the table, she felt Beth move closer, her breath soft against Nicky's cheek. To her disgust she immediately responded, warming inside, melting with love.

"I'm cooking tonight. Shrimp stir-fry. You can entertain me with conversation and act as sous chef." Beth began removing the contents of the bags. "What did you do last night?"

"Went to a show and to the Cabaret." Nicky took the shrimp to the sink to peel them.

"Wish I could go to the Cabaret sometime," she said wistfully.

"I wish you could too. I'd like to dance with you instead of Meg or somebody else."

"You danced?" Beth asked casually.

"Meg's a good dancer." She rubbed it in. "Actually, today was okay because she was here most of the day."

Silence followed this remark, then Beth took the shrimp out of Nicky's hands. "Never mind these now. Let's put them in the refrigerator. They'll keep."

"Aren't you hungry?"

Beth was leading her toward the bedroom. "Yes, but I think we need some clarification here."

"Always the lawyer," Nicky said, her face covered by the tank top Beth was pulling over her head.

Beth removed her own shorts and shirt and dropped them to the floor with Nicky's discarded clothing. Then, pushing Nicky back on the bed, she covered her with her body. "Let's get this straight, okay? You're my woman unless you tell me otherwise."

For some reason, those words shot a small thrill through Nicky. Still, she asked, "And does that mean you're mine, that you don't fuck anyone else?" She couldn't bring herself to use Mark's name.

"That means I don't make love with any other woman."

Nicky struggled to escape Beth's weight, but they were an unequal match. Beth lifted weights at the health club next to her office, and Nicky exercised irregularly — usually long walks on nice days with her camera. Lately, it had been too hot even for that. She panted, breathless from the effort. "Not fair. You can't tell me who I can and can't fuck, not while you're unfaithful."

Beth became still. "Does that mean you're going to do it with Meg?"

"I don't know. She hasn't asked me. She has Denise." Feeling Beth's fingers between her legs, she knew, even before she saw Beth's telling smile, that she was very wet. Who wouldn't be, she thought as Beth slid down her length and off the edge of the bed. When she felt the warm, gentle touch of tongue, she wrapped her legs around Beth's head.

Back in the kitchen they both wore shorts without panties and undershirts without bras. Nicky finished peeling the shrimp while Beth prepared vegetables at the cutting board. Through the open window Nicky could see the huge, golden orb of sun about to drop below the treetops. Glancing at Beth, she said quietly, "I feel at peace."

"Me too," Beth murmured.

"How much do you think good sex has to do with it?"

"It's more than sex. I suppose it has to do with feeling loved too."

"I won't argue with that," Nicky said, "but I

don't think you can have good sex without love." It was developing into one of their typical after-sex conversations.

"Surely you've had one without the other."

Meaning, Nicky supposed, that Beth had good sex with Mark. "Do you still love him?" She didn't turn away from the window, but she heard Beth sigh.

"Yes, I love him."

"And, yes, you have good sex with him?"

A deeper sigh followed. "It's different." Beth came up behind Nicky to wrap her in an embrace. "I can't explain why."

Nicky decided not to pursue it. "Let me finish peeling these little buggers, okay? I'm starved." The phone by the door rang, and they jumped. "My hands are smelly. You get it."

After listening for a few minutes, Beth sounded annoyed. "You take care of it or we'll handle it in the morning." She listened again, then said, "Let me talk to Matt."

Nicky heard the words with a sinking heart. "You can leave, you know," she said when Beth hung up.

"I'm not leaving. I can't let clients govern my life. This real piece of slime is in jail and wants out. Let Mark take care of it. He's the one who agreed to represent him. Matthew can stay with the neighbors for an hour or so. He's over there all the time anyway."

But the evening lay in ruins for Nicky. She ate without tasting and only came to life when they went back to bed, when Beth coaxed her into a reluctant passion.

III

Margo was gone for a week's vacation, leaving Nicky in charge of the Art Barn. The store activities, except for matting and framing, bored Nicky. She often read behind the counter when there was nothing else to do. Today rain fell so hard that drops bounced on contact, thunder crashed and lightning streaked across the sky. What with all the noise, she barely heard the door jangle open and looked up with surprise when Mark stood at the counter. His hair, flattened by the rain, clung to his scalp and water rolled off his raincoat.

An involuntary flush spread up Nicky's body, working its way to her face. Even her eyes burned, and she had a difficult time meeting his steady gaze. She jumped to her feet and the book slid off her lap to the floor.

"Reading on the job?" He lifted dark bushy eyebrows and smiled.

Only then did she realize he knew nothing of the love affair, that he wasn't in the store because of it. She forced a smile. "Looking for something?"

"I need help picking out a fifteen year anniversary gift for Beth. And I thought you might be just the person to give me some advice."

She had never thought of him as a handsome man. His features were much too rugged. If faces were indicative of professions, she would have guessed him to be a logger or boxer, or even a farmer. He was fit, too, filling out his tall frame with muscles. She knew he and Beth went to the health club together. Did the family who exercised together stay together?

"Did you have a painting in mind or a sculpture or some pottery?" she asked, moving out from behind the counter. Ironic that he should come to her, she thought. If she had a say in it, she'd put an end to his and Beth's anniversaries.

"What do you think?" he asked, a faint smile twitching the ends of his full lips.

"She was in here the other day with Matt but she didn't look around."

"She likes your photographs. She said you have some very nice prints for sale."

Nicky didn't want to complicate her love for Beth by liking Mark any more than she already did. She told herself that he was just acting out Beth's interest in her prints, not his own.

"Do you want to show me some?" he asked.

Realizing that she had been staring at him, she looked away in confusion. "Sure." Thunder shook the building and lightning momentarily turned the dark day white. Rain pelted the roof.

He followed her, talking. "I think we're all going to be washed away. I hear you have some animal additions to your farm. Matt told me about a shaggy dog and the horse with the strange name." Their footsteps echoed off the wood floors, a counterpoint to the rain falling on the roof.

She had been thinking that she should put on some music. Margo believed in mellowing the customers with classical music, saying it encouraged them to buy good art. "I guess he sort of looks like peanut brittle, like his name. Meg thought Matt rode real well."

"So Beth said. I think she was more excited about it than he was."

They had reached the photography section. Most of the prints were her own. He stood before them, his hands clasped behind his back. She went back to the counter and turned on the compact disk player. A Bach piano concerto competed for their attention with the thunder and pouring rain. Returning to where he stood, she tried to see her photography through his eyes.

"This one, a bolt of lightning and distant rain, it's terrific." He leaned forward to read the title, *Summer Storm*.

"Thanks," she murmured, recalling the hot day

last summer, the violent storm rapidly engulfing her, forcing her to seek shelter in the barn. Today reminded her of that time, the same frightening intensity.

There were many other framed enlargements of her work: sailboats racing on Lake Winnebago, a fiery red maple alone in a field on a cloudy fall day, day lilies along a roadside, bittersweet bushes sheathed in ice, snow on evergreens under a blue sky, a full moon setting at sunrise. She remembered taking all of them as if she had done it yesterday.

"I think I want to buy *Summer Storm* and the one called *Moon at Daybreak.*"

A bonanza, she thought. But could she do this? "Beth is my best friend," she blurted.

He turned and smiled. "Then it's appropriate for her to have some of your photographs."

"But she shouldn't have to buy them," Nicky protested, wishing he weren't so nice. No wonder Beth couldn't or wouldn't leave him.

"She isn't buying them. I am. Do you have anything to wrap them in?"

Before he left Nicky asked, "When are you celebrating?"

"Saturday." He wiggled his eyebrows and smiled suggestively. A strange, hot sensation shot through her. She had never experienced such conflicting feelings — jealousy, guilt, sympathy, admiration for him, love for his wife. So, she knew Beth wouldn't be spending Saturday with her.

Meg called her at work later that day. "Have you been home since this storm broke?"

"I can't leave until five. Why?"

"Look, I can't get out there this evening. Will you check on Brittle? If you need to get hold of me, call me at home."

The rain had slowed but still fell steadily when the truck splashed down the driveway. Scrappy didn't greet her, nor did she see Brittle. She made a run for the barn, entering by way of the milk room. The dog cowered in a corner under the blanket covering Meg's saddle. Her last dog had been afraid of storms too.

"You want to come inside?" He skulked toward her, head and tail hanging, only to jump and rush back to his safe place when distant thunder sounded. "Just let me look at Brittle," she told him.

The horse, grazing in the pasture, came running at the sight of her. Mud flew in all directions under his hooves. The area between the barn and the pasture was a thick brown sea. She poured some grain for him inside his shelter.

Tucking Scrappy under her arm, since he refused to go out into the storm, she ran with him to the house. She had looked forward to getting home and curling up with a good book. But she found she had left a few windows open and there were lakes in those rooms. Shutting the windows, she galloped down the basement stairs to look for the mop and bucket and was met with water up to the second step.

After running back out to the barn to get the hose and submersible pump from the milk room, she put on boots and got the pump going and then used most of her towels to wipe the upstairs.

By the time the wood floors were dry and she was satisfied that the pump in the basement was getting the water out, the rain had stopped. Now that she had time to sit, she found she couldn't concentrate on anything. She put her book down and listened to music, one hand resting on the dog by her side. He had emerged as soon as the thunder stopped from wherever he had been hiding.

Beth called. "I'm working late, sweetie. I thought I'd touch base to see how your day went? Anything float away out there?"

She told Beth how she had spent the hours since she had come home. She did not tell her about Mark. "You the only one at the office?"

"Yep. Working on a case. If I'd known how many undesirable characters I would have to defend, I'd have chosen some other profession." She laughed. "Any interesting news?"

"I sold a couple more prints today," Nicky remarked slyly.

"Someone has good taste. Look, I can't come out Saturday but I'll be there Sunday for sure."

Later, feeling lonely, she wandered to the porch and watched the setting sun turn the gray cloud cover yellow. The rain had cooled things off, so she put on sweatpants and a sweatshirt and walked aimlessly around the house. Scrappy shadowed her footsteps.

Meg pounded on the back door early Saturday. "I didn't want to wake Denise up, so I snuck out without coffee."

"Won't she be pissed?" Nicky asked. She filled Meg's coffee cup and her own, spooning sugar and pouring milk into hers. She ran fingers through her unkempt hair. Meg had gotten her out of bed, and she had thrown on a thin T-shirt and shorts stacked on top of a pile of clean clothes. She knew her nipples showed through the shirt.

"Oh, she'll be mad, but she'd be mad if I went off without her anyway. So I just left a note. It's easier that way." Meg stared at Nicky's breasts. "I see you took the dog in."

Flustered, Nicky sat down and covered her chest with crossed arms. She nodded. "Now that I did somebody will probably claim him."

"You mean now that you want him." Meg sipped her coffee. "I tell you it's the pits to lie. The thing is you have to remember everything you say or you get caught."

"I suppose. So tell her the truth."

Meg looked horrified. "She'd kill me." A grin stole across her face. "She thinks there's somebody else in my life."

"Then she'll be relieved to find out that 'somebody' is only Brittle."

"That's what you think."

"Well, you know her better than I do," Nicky said. She was almost glad she wasn't involved in a live-in relationship. "Beth can't make it today, so Matt won't be here either."

"Damn," Meg said quietly. "I didn't need to sneak out this morning."

"You don't have to stay."

"Can I use your phone? I'll just give Denise a call."

Nicky, listening discreetly, cleaned up the dishes while Meg talked.

"I'll be home this afternoon. I thought I had to work. I got my messages confused, I guess." Meg looked tense. "I don't know why they told you that. I was there briefly. Now I've got some errands to run. You want anything at the store?" She breathed a relieved sigh when she hung up the phone. "She's madder than hell. She called work and I wasn't there, of course."

"Do you have to tell her wherever you go?" Nicky asked, wiping the counter with a dishcloth.

"On weekends it's hard to get away alone. She thinks we should be together." Meg slumped in a chair.

"Well, that's sort of the idea of a relationship," Nicky said. "Are you sure you should be in one?"

Stretching her long legs in front of her, Meg shrugged her shoulders. "Getting out isn't so easy. It's easier not to get involved. Besides, I love her." She pulled herself together and placed her hands palms down on the maple surface. "It's a nice day. I'll give you a lesson if you like."

Nicky laughed. "No thanks."

The outdoors had been washed clean. Leaves and grass and weeds no longer looked dusty and drooping, but instead were colored bright green. Nicky knew she would have to mow again this weekend, even though she had cut the lawn less than a week ago. Weeds proliferated in the garden, hiding the vegetables planted beneath them.

"I'd like to show Brittle," Meg said as they walked toward the barn.

"Show him where?"

"At open horse shows, or even Quarter Horse shows." Meg added, "He has hundreds of Quarter

Horse points. He may not look like it, covered with mud and out of shape, but he's a show horse."

Nicky eyed Brittle with renewed interest as Meg tied him to the post and started currying the mud off him. "How would you do that? Wouldn't you have to tell Denise?"

Snorting, Meg said, "I suggested this to Denise once before. We had the biggest battle of our lives."

"Well, I don't see how you can do it without telling her. When are these shows?"

"On the weekends, and I don't own a truck or trailer." Meg looked dejected. "Here's the chance of a lifetime and I can't take advantage of it."

Nicky wasn't stupid. She knew Meg was asking her to help with this scheme. And she realized with surprise that she might want to be part of it. Western art, horse art, sold. She could do a horse show series. But she only said, "You'll have to tell her."

Meg sounded panicked. "I'm a coward." With the curry comb she pulverized the clods of dried mud hanging on the horse's coat until she and Brittle were enveloped in a cloud of dust. The horse hung his head as if he enjoyed the grooming. After a while, Meg said in measured tones, "What I think I'll do is tell her I'm going home a few weekends. She won't call my folks. They don't get along. Then, if we have some success, I'll talk to her."

"It's a mistake," Nicky warned, curious to meet this woman who intimidated Meg so.

"Is Beth coming out tomorrow?" Meg asked.

Meg was cleaning Brittle's feet, which Nicky equated to picking someone else's toes. She wrinkled her nose. "Yes, but she won't bring Matt with her."

Meg set the hoof down and moved to another one. "Why is that?"

"Because she won't." She better not, Nicky thought. By Sunday Nicky would need some serious loving.

The next day, as they walked through the pasture, Nicky told Beth about Meg's plans. Meg rode Brittle at the far end of the fenced-in acreage. Nicky felt she had lost the field to Brittle. She was afraid to even walk to the stream unless Meg had the horse in hand. Meg had started Brittle's conditioning the day before. There was an open show next Saturday and Meg wanted to go. Nicky had offered herself and her truck. Meg just had to rent a horse trailer.

"Sure you want to do that? This Denise could make trouble," Beth said.

Even though she'd thought that herself, Nicky became defensive. "It'll be something to do on Saturday anyway."

Beth changed tack. "I hung your prints in the living room. What a lovely gift. It's like having you in the house."

"The next best thing to being there," Nicky said nastily, recalling the niceness of Mark and feeling like a shit all over again. She glanced at Beth, who stood next to her staring into the tumbling water, holding herself tightly with crossed arms. She touched her. "Beth." Seeing tears in Beth's eyes, Nicky's anger melted. "Don't, Beth."

Sniffing and wiping her wet face with the heel of her hand, Beth laughed shakily. "Sorry. I understand your anger. I just don't know how to change things."

"Come on." Nicky tugged at Beth's hand, pulled her down into the tall grass next to the creek. She pushed Scrappy out of the way and stretched out beside her. "It seems like I'm forgetting how to enjoy you when you're here." She kissed the corner of Beth's trembling mouth. "Want to do it?"

"Here? Now?" She rolled on her side and wrapped Nicky in her arms. "Yes."

They reached inside each other's shorts and gently caressed the sensitive folds of flesh, eliciting so much pleasure that Nicky was only vaguely aware of the whining dog and the buzzing insects. She rode Beth's touch on a mounting wave of excitement, unable to curb for long the passion surging through her.

"That's what you call a quickie," Nicky murmured, as they pulled their clothes into a semblance of order and smiled somewhat sheepishly at each other.

Beth lay with her arms under her head. She turned her face toward Nicky and said almost shyly, "I forget the slime I was so eager to represent when I'm with you. I wish I could come home to you, Nicky."

Nicky plucked a stem of grass and chewed on it. She sat cross-legged next to her. "It's okay, Beth." But she knew that what made it okay right now had been the sex and the tears. "Besides, you take your work home with Mark. Too bad he's such a nice guy."

Putting a blade of grass between her teeth, Beth frowned. "I got the feeling I was being followed when I came out today."

"One of the slime?" Nicky asked, her voice rising in alarm and her scalp crawling.

"It was probably just my imagination." She smiled reassuringly. "Why would any of my clients follow me? I'm supposedly helping them, although I'd like some put away for good. Maybe I should run for prosecutor." She grinned, showing beautiful white teeth.

"I'd vote for that smile, and then I'd fuck you senseless."

Beth laughed. "I'll have to smile more often."

When Beth left late that night, Nicky saw headlights turn on further down the road, as if a car had been parked there. She watched the lights approach her driveway then pass it, taking the direction the Probe had taken. Starting her truck, she backed around and sped after Beth, catching up with her as she turned onto Highway 41. There was no one tailing her. Still, she followed her to a Super America and pulled in behind her.

"I thought that was you," Beth said, opening her gas tank. "Couldn't you wait until tomorrow to fill up, or did you just miss me?" Wisps of hair blew around her face, catching in the corners of her mouth and eyes.

"I thought you were being tailed," Nicky said, feeling foolish. "Did you see a car turn on its lights and follow you when you left my driveway?"

"I did see a car behind me, but it turned off a block or so before forty-one." She brushed the loose hair away from her face.

Not totally convinced, Nicky asked, "Want me to follow you home?" She shut off the gas pump and screwed the cap on.

"Thanks, sweetie, but I'll be fine."

Nicky watched Beth drive away from the gas station. When she saw no car in pursuit, she drove slowly home with the windows open, enjoying the soft breeze on her face, the sky full of stars, the growing concert of insects.

IV

"Why doesn't Denise get along with your folks?" Nicky asked.

"She told them we were lovers when she went home with me." Meg studied the map on her lap. "And they told her we weren't."

"You're kidding," Nicky said in hushed tones, horrified and amused and almost disbelieving.

Meg laughed humorlessly. "They said they wanted to hear it from me. I tried to be honest. I just couldn't. They ordered Denise out of the house."

"Did you go with her?"

Meg nodded. "She was furious with me. I didn't see my parents for a year, and then I visited them without Denise. It's better that way." She looked at Nicky. "They aren't going to live forever."

"Why did she tell them?" Nicky asked, trying to imagine such a scene.

"You gotta know my parents and Denise. They're a couple of bigots and she's righteous, which is almost as bad." Meg pointed to the right. "Turn there. That's the fairgrounds."

They parked under a tree at the edge of the gravel parking lot, and Meg unloaded Brittle and tied him to the trailer.

"You ever done this before?" Nicky asked, looking at the horses in the arena. They were lined up in a long row with their handlers next to them. A man in a Western-type suit and cowboy hat walked around the animals.

"I've shown Brittle a few times." Meg gave the horse a cursory brushing. She had already spent hours getting him ready.

Nicky had been surprised by the time-consuming preparations. She had seen Meg clip the horse, wash him, clean her tack. Now she stood by while Meg readied him to ride and took him to where others were working their horses. With her camera she wandered the fairgrounds, absorbing the show in progress and those getting ready to show. She sat in the bleachers during the noon break while everyone rode in the arena. Afterwards, she watched the riding classes.

When Meg's class entered the ring for Senior Western Pleasure, Nicky went to the fence and snapped frames of her as she rode past. At first she hardly recognized her, dressed in Western hat and chaps and boots, her long sleeves rolled down and buttoned, a scarf pinned at her neck. Meg made a face at her during the first pass, said something Nicky missed during the second. Nicky paid so much attention to Meg that she forgot to watch Brittle.

On the way home Nicky silently added up the day's expenses. The charge at the gate, for entrance to the show grounds, had been two dollars each. The classes had cost Meg seven dollars apiece to enter. She had paid for trailer rental and gas. Nicky thought it had been an expensive day for Meg to be so pleased over Brittle's fourth-place winning.

Already Meg was talking about going to another show next Saturday. Nicky wasn't sure she wanted to do this every weekend and started to say so, but Meg spoke first. "I forgot to ask. Can I spend the night at your place? Denise doesn't expect me home until tomorrow."

"Won't she be glad to have you home?"

"Yeah, but she'll make me go to a chamber music concert with her at Lawrence tomorrow."

"What if she finds out you stayed with me?" Nicky asked, realizing she might be more afraid of Denise than the slime Beth represented.

Dreaming that Beth was climbing into bed with her, Nicky murmured and obligingly moved over. She snuggled against her. It had been so long since she and Beth had slept together that she had forgotten how comforting it felt.

She woke to a lonely bed, so certain she had not

spent the night alone that she touched the other side. "Beth, you out there?" she called. Not even the dog came running. He'd started the night beside the bed. The clock read eight thirty-five. Stripes of sunlight fell across the rumpled sheets. She threw off the tangled top sheet, pulled on a shirt and shorts and padded toward the kitchen.

Through the window she could see the dog sitting by the back door and Meg out in the horse lot pitching manure into a wheelbarrow. Meg had supposedly slept on the couch. Looking at the sheets and blanket neatly folded where she had placed them for Meg's use last night, Nicky felt hot liquid flowing through her veins.

Scrappy jumped all over her when she went outside, his toenails scratching her bare legs. Impatiently pushing him down with her knee, she stretched in the already hot sunlight. Uncertain of what to do next, she sat on the stoop and patted the dog. Meg looked different to her. Disturbingly sexual images came to mind — Meg's breasts bouncing against her cotton T-shirt, the damp spots under and between them, the long tightly muscled legs.

Grabbing her camera, Nicky started blindly down the road. Surprised, she realized that she had reached the next farm. Dan was cutting alfalfa in the field next to the driveway. Swallows, iridescent and graceful, soared and dove for the insects stirred up by the tractor and mower. She raised her camera and caught the farmer on film, the tractor at work, the birds accompanying them. At the far end of the field Dan lifted a hand in acknowledgment.

Even before she started reluctantly toward home, Scrappy urged her in that direction with his nose against her leg. Half hoping that Meg would be gone or at least riding, she walked slowly through the hazy, hot, late morning. The sun beat down with an intensity that sapped energy from plants and animals. She photographed Scrappy standing in a ditch full of purple vetch, then snapped fields of hawkweed, bright orange in the sunny day, with blue spiderwort growing amidst its profusion.

The Rabbit was gone from the driveway. Parked in its place were Beth's Probe, Nicky's father's Jeep Grand Wagoneer, and her sister Natalie's old beat-up Plymouth Horizon. Her heart jumped and then fell. As usual, her parents had not informed her of their intent to visit. She sometimes thought they got into their car on Sundays never knowing where they would end up.

They were sitting in lawn chairs under the sugar maple near the back door. Nicky became aware of her old shorts and shirt, her beat up tennis shoes. She ran fingers through the hair she had washed but hadn't combed that morning. Unprotected by makeup or suntan lotion, her face felt burned. She had always longed to carry herself as her mother did, with unconscious grace.

"Five for dinner?" she asked with a slight smile, worried that her family would leave too late to allow her time alone with Beth.

Her father wrapped her in a bear hug and she sniffed his familiar smell. "You're bony, Nick." He was tall and hardy, casually attired in expensive clothes, with thick graying dark hair and a ready smile.

"I'm fine, Dad. I eat like a horse. Which reminds me, did you see the horse?"

"Yes dear." Her mother looked chic, as always. A slender woman with prematurely white hair cut short to emphasize high cheekbones and dark blue eyes like her own, she rose from her chair to give Nicky a kiss on the cheek and a squeeze.

Nicky briefly studied her twenty-year-old sister, who was a sullen, heavier version of herself. "Haven't seen you for a while, little sister. What've you been up to?"

"No good," Natalie said without a change of expression.

Nicky laughed. "You'll have to tell me about it."

She turned to Beth, elegant in hair and clothing, slim and lovely, and thought that she should be her mother's daughter, not herself or her sister. She gave her a radiant smile. "Hello, and what did you bring?" Beth had promised to grocery shop.

"Makings for cashew chicken." Beth smiled hesitantly, and Nicky knew that she was thinking of leaving.

"You'll have to fix it," Nicky said flatly, allowing her no polite way out.

"If you insist," Beth replied.

"I'm sure we could manage, dear," Nicky's mother began.

"No, we couldn't, Mom," Nicky assured her, "but it sure is good to see you." She put an arm around her mother's waist and walked with her toward the door. Scrappy followed them into the house.

"Got yourself another dog?" her dad asked, bending nearly double to scratch behind the drooping ears.

"Scrappy found me," Nicky said.

"Ward, I left my purse in the car. Would you get

it for me?" her mother asked, as they milled around the kitchen.

He boomed, "Sure, honey. I want to take a look at that horse anyway. Why don't you come with me, Nattie?"

Sensing a setup, she asked, "Something going on, Mom?"

Her mother sat at the table and fanned herself with a paper plate. "How do you stand this heat, Nicole? We could help you with the cost of air conditioning. Just a window unit would make a difference."

"That's very generous, Mom," Nicky said automatically. Her parents were always offering her financial assistance. When desperate, she had been forced to accept it. "I like open windows." She turned to help Beth, who was cutting chicken breasts into strips.

"That's okay," Beth said, giving her a heart-stopping smile. "Talk to your mother. You don't see her that often."

Nicky remarked, "Nice to see Natalie. She doesn't usually come with you."

"Well, it's not her choice to be here today. Your father and I wanted to ask you if your sister could stay with you this summer. She's got a lot of reading to do, a lot of catching up, in order to pass some tests in the fall. Otherwise, she'll have to leave the university."

Nicky stared at her mother, remembering her own leave-taking from the university. Continuing had seemed pointless after Beth had married. The only enduring interest she had at the time was photography.

Her concerns were selfish ones. She considered what Natalie's presence would do to her social life, her sex life. How could she explain what was going on? Turning toward Beth, she met her eyes and read the worry in them.

She had never been close to Natalie. Fifteen years separated them, but Nicky had never experienced the maternal feelings she knew some older sisters have toward their younger siblings.

Her mother said worriedly, "Your father and I are at the end of our wits with what to do with her. She drinks. We think she uses marijuana."

Strangling the laugh rising up her throat, Nicky said, "Mom, every kid does some marijuana these days. What would I do with her? I can't make her listen to me."

"Put her to work. Mowing, working in the garden, putting up vegetables, even taking care of the horse."

"Meg takes care of Brittle," Nicky muttered, feeling out of sorts. She sat down and put her chin in her hand. She wanted desperately to discuss the request with Beth. "Let me think about it. Okay?"

Her mother sighed. "All right, Nicole, but don't think long. She's packed and ready to stay. It took a lot of convincing to get her here. She said you wouldn't want her."

Nicky stiffened. Her mother's sighs had never ceased to bother her. "Want a cup of coffee?" she asked.

"In this heat? How about a glass of iced tea?"

"Coming up." She took a pitcher out of the refrigerator. "Want one, Beth?"

There was no chance to discuss with Beth Natalie's staying. Feeling as if she had once more been bowled over by her parents, Nicky agreed to take her little sister in. She even accepted a generous check from her father for the cost of putting her up. She thought grimly that her financial woes were solved, but the solution might be worse than the problem.

Nicky gave Natalie an upstairs bedroom. "Terrific," she muttered as she watched her sister drag an enormous suitcase up the stairs. For the first time that day, she and Beth were alone.

Beth smiled wryly. "Looks like it's going to be a long hot summer."

"Come on," Nicky said, taking Beth by the hand, leading her to the barn. They slipped through the large double doors and climbed the ladder to the hay mow. Nicky placed an old blanket on the prickly straw and hay strewn across the floor. She smiled into Beth's hazel eyes. "It's the best I can do."

"I'm not this desperate," Beth said, sneezing at the dust floating in the evening air. A few flies buzzed lazily in the nearly horizontal rays of sun leaking through the gaps in the warped siding.

"Come on. What's the difference between here and the field. It's all grass. This is just drier." Nicky dropped to her knees, heard them crack. She tugged at Beth until she joined her. "I'm sorry, Beth. I still can't say no to my parents."

"You're conditioned, sweetie." Beth kissed her on the mouth.

"I know." Nicky lay on her side, taking Beth down with her. The hay and straw poked her through the blanket.

Beth murmured into Nicky's mouth, "I thought I was too old for uncomfortable sex."

Nicky unbuttoned Beth's shirt and breathed softly on her nipples through the white cotton undershirt. She didn't remove Beth's clothing or her own. It offered some protection from the uncomfortable bedding. Instead, she reached inside Beth's underwear to caress her into passionate response.

When Nicky returned to the house, having seen Beth off, she found her sister on the living room couch with the television on. Nicky seldom watched TV during the warm months, although she sometimes buried herself in movies in the dark cold of winter. "What are you watching?"

Natalie grunted. "I don't even know."

"Can we turn it off then? Put on some music?" When her sister shrugged indifferently, Nicky turned on the CD player.

Natalie groaned at the classical music. "You got any Springsteen?" she asked.

"I've got Bonnie Raitt," Nicky said, changing the CD. She started for the porch with Scrappy close on her heels. "I'm going out here. Want to join me?" She stretched full-length on the chaise lounge and smiled in the dark when Natalie plodded after her.

"That dog has a bad case of the cutes," her sister said, plopping onto a lawn chair.

Nicky laughed a little. "I think he knows it, too." She realized that she hardly knew this young woman, even though she had known her all her life. "Mom said you have a lot of reading to do," she said quietly, thinking that the darkness protected them from each other.

"I do if I'm going to stay at the university. You never graduated."

Nicky could feel Natalie's eyes on her. "I know,"

she murmured. "All I ever wanted to do was take pictures. What is it you want to do?"

The girl snorted. "Who knows?"

"Well, what do you like to do?"

"Cook. Your friend? Beth? She's a good cook. But I'm better," she stated flatly.

Nicky smiled to herself, quite willing never to fix another meal. "Then you can cook for us. Do you like to do anything else? Clean? Garden? Mow? Take care of horses?"

"Gonna use me for slave labor?"

"Yes," Nicky said, pleased when her sister's laughter joined her own.

The next morning, Monday, Nicky left a note for Natalie on the kitchen table—a list of things that needed to be done. Scrappy chased her truck to the end of the driveway before turning back.

Her vacation over, a sunburned Margo took care of the counter. Nicky closeted herself in the back room with the large number of framing orders. With the radio on and a pot of coffee by her side, she worked nonstop until five-thirty, and then only quit because Natalie was at the house.

Parking next to the Rabbit, still unsure of how to greet Meg, she was relieved to see her riding in the pasture. She headed for the house to change her clothes and reached the back door before realizing what was missing. Scrappy was nowhere to be seen. Opening the screen door, she entered the empty house.

She changed from cotton slacks and blouse to

shorts and tank top and went back outdoors. Meg was riding toward the barn with easy grace, her body moving with the horse's rhythm. Nicky took a deep breath and walked to meet her through the long grass. Brittle swished his tail and stomped his feet at the flies he attracted.

"I met your sister. She looks a lot like you," Meg said.

"I suppose. She has the same color hair and eyes. Do you know where she is? Scrappy isn't even around."

"I saw them go off down the road a couple hours ago. They'll be back. She here for a visit?"

"She's here for the summer," Nicky said with a short laugh, working the ground with the toe of one tennis shoe.

"Really? How nice." Meg smiled, her face rosy in the sun. "You disappeared Sunday morning. I had to leave before you came back." She ran a hand along the side of Brittle's long neck.

Nicky's face grew hot and she looked away. It felt like an invasion of privacy to suspect that someone had been in bed with her without her knowledge or consent. She took a deep breath and decided to confront the issue head-on. "You didn't sleep on the couch Saturday night, did you?" She squinted up at Meg who had the sun behind her, turning her ash blonde hair golden.

Meg's smile became mischievous. "So you knew?"

"No, I didn't know. I guessed." She tried to sound annoyed. "Don't do that again."

"I'll ask next time."

"Don't ask either. I'm involved."

Brittle rested a hind foot, shifting Meg's weight.

He tried to lower his head to graze, but Meg lifted the reins. "I know. With Beth, who's married."

Scrappy shot out of the grass like a small black missile and bounced off Nicky's legs. Startled, she pushed him away and saw her sister walking toward them.

"Checking out the neighborhood?" Nicky inquired.

"I was down the road at Dan's. He gave me a ride on his tractor. Nice guy."

"Yeah, he is," Nicky said.

"I did everything on the list, except the mowing. I'll do that tomorrow if you'll show me how to start the mower. Neil always does it at home."

The names of Nicky's siblings all began with *N*. Besides Neil and herself and Natalie, there was Nancy, who was married and had two children. Nicky wondered if her parents had planned the five years between each of their offspring, just as they had chosen names with the same first letter.

She also wondered if they had given their children ordinary names because their own names were unusual. Her father, Ward, carried his mother's maiden name. Her grandfather had nicknamed his daughter Cleo, because she behaved like a little queen. She still did, Nicky thought.

Natalie said to Meg, "You promised me a ride. I'm going to hold you to it."

Meg jumped to the ground, and Natalie grabbed the front of the saddle and the horn, put one foot in the stirrup, and struggled up. "Man, it's a long way down," she said, looking nervous.

"I'll lead him." Meg continued on foot toward the barn.

Wanting to be alone, Nicky headed for the creek.

Scrappy disappeared in the long growth ahead of her. Queen Anne's lace bobbed over the tops of the tall grasses, which bent in shimmering waves before the evening breeze.

V

Tan and robust, looking freshly scrubbed and clad in clean jeans and shirt, Dan appeared at the back door on Friday evening. Nicky greeted him with surprise. She didn't mean to be rude. She just didn't know what to make of his presence until Natalie showed up, also dressed to go out.

"You're early," Natalie said.

He grinned broadly. "Am I? I can go home and start over."

Nicky stepped back from them. She felt foolish

and a little miffed, wondering why Natalie hadn't told her to expect him. "Come on in, Dan."

He sat at the kitchen table for a few minutes of friendly talk. "You want to go with us?" he asked Nicky.

Nicky, who was cleaning up after Natalie's cooking, cringed at his polite offer. "Thanks, but I have plans. I just didn't know you and Natalie had a date."

"Kind of quick, huh?" He grinned again, looking slightly silly.

"Well, I don't know about that. I don't know how often you see each other. I'm gone all day."

His smile vanished as he sought to reassure her. "Oh, we just talk while I work. Sometimes we talk while she works."

Nicky couldn't accuse her sister of not doing her fair share. Natalie had done everything asked of her. She heard them drive off in Dan's Chevy truck. Imagining her mother's reaction to this latest development, she mentally prepared her own defense. She had warned her mother that she couldn't control her sister.

Scrappy lay near the door — a heap of hair with no evident beginning or end. She had lied, having planned nothing for the evening. Beth was with her family; Meg was probably with Denise. There were only casual friends and acquaintances to call. She had let close friendships fall by the wayside while waiting for Beth to fill her weekends. During the intervening six years between Beth's marriage and the resumption of their affair, Nicky had taken three lovers — none very satisfying or long lasting.

Calling the dog to go with her to feed Brittle, she

realized that Meg had not fulfilled her promise to always care for the horse. More often than not, Nicky fed him. She had even picked up grain for him during the week, for which Meg had promised to reimburse her. But although she had seen Meg twice since, she hadn't forked over any money. Nicky wondered if she would pay next month's board on time. Meg and Natalie planned to attend a horse show together Sunday. Dan had offered to haul Brittle in his stock trailer. Now Nicky understood why.

Brittle always came running at feeding time, which never failed to alarm her. She dumped the grain into the feed tub from behind the safety of the fence whenever possible. When it wasn't, she rushed in and out of the enclosure. Scrappy barked and snapped, posturing from a distance. Wisely, he kept out of Brittle's reach.

As Nicky stood watching the horse eat, Meg drove in. Fending off Scrappy's friendly welcome, she joined Nicky at the fence.

"I didn't expect you tonight." Nicky smiled, pleased to have company.

"I didn't expect me either, but I got paid today." She handed Nicky the money she owed her for grain. "And Denise is gone again for the weekend." She rested her arms on the top of the fence and eyed Brittle critically. "I think he looks better, more in shape. Don't you?"

Nicky looked at Meg. "He looks terrific."

Meg threw an arm around her, gave her a squeeze. "Thanks for taking him in. I've watched horses come and go. I don't care what anybody says. They know when they've been sold and are distressed when they have to leave friends and familiar surroundings. As big as they are, they have no control over their lives."

"He doesn't have any friends here," Nicky pointed out.

"That's what I was getting to," Meg continued. "He needs a companion."

Nicky was wary. "Another horse?"

"I know a nice pony that's for sale. Maybe Beth would like to buy him for Matt."

"You'll have to suggest that to her."

"Is she going to bring Matt out tomorrow?"

"She said she was."

They drove to look at the pony the next day. Nicky and Matt sat in the back of Beth's Probe, hot wind washing over them from the open sunroof. Matt talked nonstop.

Prancing in his stall, the pony nickered excitedly. To Nicky he looked like a horse. His eyes were large and prominent, his neck crested, his body long and narrow. Named Sweet Tater, perhaps for his deep red coat, he was big enough for Meg to ride. She put Matt on his back when she got off.

While Matt jounced around the small enclosure on Tater, Meg prevailed upon Beth. "It's hard to find a good pony. You want him to move like a horse and this one does. You want him to be gentle and kind like Tater here. I can give Matt lessons on the pony instead of on Brittle, and in time, maybe we can go to the open shows together."

Nicky thought Meg had missed her calling. She should have been a saleswoman, persuading even Nicky that Tater would be a good investment.

"I'll think about it," Beth promised.

But Matthew begged for the pony, and Beth finally gave in. With Tater came his tack. They promised to pick him up the first of the week. The pony whinnied when they left his small barn. Nicky wondered if he called from loneliness and smiled when Matthew patted his neck, promising to return for him.

Meg stayed late enough that night that Nicky didn't object when she suggested she sleep on the couch. "Why go home now when I have to get up so early in the morning?" Natalie had gone to her room earlier in the evening and left them alone on the porch, where Meg had cleaned tack for tomorrow's show.

Stretching, Nicky undressed in her bedroom and crawled between the sheets.

"I appreciate this," Meg called from the other room.

"S'okay," Nicky murmured before falling asleep.

She woke late to Scrappy barking. Walking barefoot through the house, Nicky looked through the windows and saw Brittle clamber into Dan's trailer, watched Meg climb into the truck with Dan and Natalie and drive away. She and Beth would have the day to themselves. They'd just have to get their loving in early.

Still dispensing heat, the evening sun skimmed distant treetops when Tater and Brittle, snorting excitement, raced to meet each other in the pasture. Nicky, with Beth's check in her pocket, thought wryly that her financial worries might really be over.

She had hoped that Beth would solve her money difficulties by moving in with her. Instead, she gave her Tater as a consolation prize. A horse, a pony and a sister to board.

Matt sat on top of a fence post. Nicky watched Natalie hoist herself into Dan's truck. As they towed the stock trailer out the driveway, Nicky wondered if they had done it yet, if that's what they did at his place. For the life of her she couldn't figure out what she should do about their mutual attraction, if anything.

Brittle dwarfed the pony, but if Tater was intimidated, he gave no indication of it. They circled each other, touched noses, snorted some more, lifted their front feet off the ground in mock rears and their rumps in half-hearted kicks, and ended up grazing side by side.

Meg relaxed her stance. "You never know if they're going to get along, but they're herd animals. They don't like to be alone." She patted Matthew on the back. "Well, cowboy, when do you want to start riding?"

"And you said he was a city boy," Nicky remarked to Beth.

Beth disarmed her with a smile. "What does a mother know?"

When Beth turned the Probe out of the driveway and Meg followed in the Rabbit, Nicky looked back toward the crossroads west of her place. Her heart leaped when she saw a car there, ominously dark against the fading light. She made an effort to establish make and model and color when it cruised slowly past her driveway in the direction Beth and

Meg had taken. She guessed it to be a Toyota Celica, judging from the taillights that resembled cat's eyes.

At the Art Barn the next day, as Nicky framed her enlargements of Meg riding Brittle, she mulled over her phone conversation with Beth last night.

Beth had been amused. "It's the artist in you, your vivid imagination. But I'll check to see what my more dangerous clients drive."

Nicky wasn't reassured. "I'm scared for you, Beth. Look in your rearview mirror."

"I will, sweetie. I promise."

Showing the newly framed photos to Margo, she told her about her planned horse series. "What do you think?" When Margo didn't comment, she persisted, "Be honest. Do you think it's a dumb idea?"

Margo took the enlargement of Meg and Brittle silhouetted against the sunset and hung it next to the red maple in the field. She spoke in a choked voice. "Things aren't good, Nicky."

"What do you mean?" Nicky asked, immediately worried.

"Victor wants a divorce." Margo's voice cracked and tears welled in her blue eyes.

Nicky reached for her friend, held the large woman against her — ashamed because she felt more concern for herself and her job than she did for Margo's pain. "I'm sorry," she said lamely.

Margo laughed bitterly. "Me too. He's got some young thing he can't let go of." She freed herself from Nicky's embrace and searched through her pockets. Nicky handed her a tissue and Margo blew her nose. "He wants to sell the building."

Nicky stood frozen, her thoughts racing. She had no training, no degree. The job at the Art Barn had been a comfortable outlet for her talents. She might even have to sell her house.

Margo dried her eyes and looked apologetically at Nicky. "I don't have a choice. I could accept the building as part of a settlement, but it would be risky. I really need to take the money and invest it."

"Have you considered counseling?" Nicky asked. Wasn't that what everyone did these days?

"He wants out." Margo sat dejectedly on the short ladder. "Look at me. Can you blame him?"

Nicky didn't think Victor was such a prize and said so.

Margo laughed, a harsh, nearly hysterical sound. "You're right there, honey, but you'll never convince him of that. He thinks he's God's gift to women."

Nicky seldom saw Victor and had never looked at him as anyone other than Margo's husband—middle-aged, affable, big but not fat. His crowning glory was his gray hair, still thick and wavy. *Philanderer,* she thought.

"Guess I better start looking for another job," she said, as much to herself as to Margo.

"I've had time to think about all of this," Margo said, looking and sounding more in control, "and I think I'll use my home as a gallery. I can show your photographs there. I wish I could do more."

"Thanks. It'll work out, Margo," Nicky said, not at all sure how. She gave Margo's shoulder a comforting squeeze. "How do you want to do this?"

"We'll just continue business as usual until there is no more business." She began crying in earnest then.

Pouring over the classifieds on the front porch after work, Nicky waited for Natalie to call her to dinner. Natalie had told Nicky that she would cook, but only if Nicky stayed out of the way. "No more Cleos in my kitchen," Natalie had said, referring to her mother by her first name. "Mom hovers. She thinks I can't do anything. But Scrappy, he can stay." Nicky felt sure that Scrappy was there right now, waiting for food fallout.

Having found no job prospects for her in the ads, Nicky folded the newspaper and tossed it on the floor. She settled back on the chaise lounge and watched the evening develop.

Normally she loved the time just before dark, when work was over and her thoughts could wander while the day quietly came to a scenic conclusion. But now she hardly heard the cardinal singing in the white pine at the edge of the yard or the crickets starting their nightly ruckus.

She had chased her thoughts aimlessly around ever since Margo's news had blown her out of the water. If worse came to worse, she could always waitress somewhere or work at a fast food place. She sighed and got a whiff of Natalie's cooking. Tonight promised a Mexican feast. Nicky had agreed without interest when Nattie suggested that Dan join them.

Dan's truck jolted down the driveway, Nicky knew that Scrappy's few barks were directed at him. She slid lower in the chaise lounge as she listened to the sounds of Dan's and Natalie's voices. Not at all sure she was up to company, she briefly thought about declining dinner, but the tantalizing odors got the best of her.

Natalie's menu included chicken fajitas, refried beans, Spanish rice. None of it came ready-made. Natalie scorned easy cooking. She often made her own bread and happily spent hours preparing food, causing Nicky to wonder where this penchant for creative cooking came from. Certainly not from their mother.

As a child, Nicky had eaten canned beans, Kraft macaroni and cheese, frozen pizza, hot dogs. It wasn't that Cleo didn't know how to cook from scratch, because Nicky had eaten fancy meals often enough, but her mother considered time spent in the kitchen as time wasted. Nicky knew that her sister, Nancy, followed her mother's example. Her dad grilled on occasion but never anything more ambitious than chicken or steak or bratwurst.

"Cutting hay again?" Nicky asked Dan between bites, consciously controlling the urge to wolf down her dinner. She had never eaten Mexican food this good.

"Mmm-hmm." His mouth full, he nodded.

Natalie bent to her plate and, with a small smile, took a bite. She looked pleased.

"The food is superb," Nicky said, putting aside her apathetic stupor over Margo's news. "Have you ever thought of starting a restaurant, Nattie?"

Natalie looked at her as if she had just noticed her presence. "What? No."

"You should talk to Dad about it. He might be willing to set you up or something. He and Mom are always trying to foist money on me. I think cooking is your calling. Aren't they paying us a visit this weekend?"

"Yes, but we're going to a show with Meg."

"Doesn't Matt have a riding lesson?" Nicky asked, feeling out of touch.

In Meg's absence, Natalie and Dan had taken over the care of Brittle, who was now being kept inside days and turned out evenings for a few hours. Meg said it would keep his coat from fading and him from getting a belly.

"Saturday morning."

"Well, I'll call Mom and tell them to come Saturday."

Natalie shrugged indifferently.

After dinner Nicky thought she would take a walk with the dog, see how Brittle and Tater were doing, and call Beth. She needed to talk to someone about what had happened today.

Lingering outside, even though most of the light was gone, she leaned against the fence while Dan turned Brittle loose. The horse thundered out of the barn to join Tater in the pasture, where they squealed and ran off together for a turn around the field. She found their head-tossing, bucking, kicking greetings disconcerting — a bit excessive, she thought, for a friendly hello.

"You going to meet the folks Saturday?" she asked Dan.

He nodded. He seemed like such a silent man. She thought it would be lonely living with him. Then he quietly said, "I think your idea about a restaurant is a good one. Why don't you suggest Nattie fix dinner Saturday night?"

"She always does. Oh, you mean something really good, something to convince the folks." She smiled slyly, relishing any underhanded attempts to direct her parents' decisions.

After Dan and Natalie disappeared together, Nicky called Beth to tell her about the inevitable loss of her job. Just saying the words made them more real to her, and she felt momentarily desperate. "I don't have any training, Beth, other than photography."

"Maybe you can work for the *Gazette.*"

"Oh sure. I don't have a degree either."

"You have experience. You're already a professional."

But Nicky thought they wouldn't see it that way at the newspaper. "I might try a photography studio."

"Do that, too. I'm sorry for Margo, but at least there'll be an outlet for your work at her place." She suggested they meet for lunch.

Saturday morning Meg caught Brittle, and Tater followed them into the enclosure. She had put a gate where the lot outside the barn opened to the pasture, and now she closed it behind herself and the two animals, then tied them both to posts. "Get in here, Matt, and clean Tater up."

While Matt and Meg worked on the animals, Nicky and Beth sat at the picnic table and drank coffee. "The 'For Sale' sign went up in front of the store yesterday. I can't believe how fast everything is moving. One day it's just talk and the next it's reality."

"It might take a while to sell, Nicky. Real estate isn't a hot item these days."

Nicky studied her coffee gloomily. "I can't seem to get moving. I need to get a resume ready."

Beth clasped Nicky's hands, which were wrapped around her cup. "I'm so sorry, sweetie."

"It's easy working at the Art Barn, hardly work at all. And it's a place to exhibit my stuff. I didn't even appreciate it."

Beth shrugged. "That's what happens. It's called taking things for granted."

Nicky grunted. "Yeah, well, I won't do it again." She looked up as the Wagoneer turned into the driveway. "Look who's here already." She got up to greet her parents.

They spent the day outside, some of it talking in the shade of the maple, some of it touring Dan's farm, some of it watching Matt and Meg ride.

When the five of them sat down to dinner, Nicky was tired. She had thrown the restaurant idea into the conversation sometime during the afternoon, after Meg and Matt and Beth left. Her parents had looked surprised, then she thought her dad appeared thoughtful.

Now Natalie placed before them roasted beef tenderloin, glazed fresh beets, mashed rutabaga, a tossed salad to be served with her own salad dressing, and homemade bread. The wine was a Napa Ridge Pinot Noir.

The smell of the food filled Nicky with hunger and hope that her restaurant idea would take hold in her parents' minds. Maybe she could wait tables and take photos of the diners, she thought wryly. She hadn't told any of them that she would soon be jobless.

They ate in silence at first, the food too good to be ignored. Then her dad raved about the beef, her mother praised the vegetables, Dan commented on the bread, and Natalie looked indifferent, saying, "There's raspberry pie for dessert."

Her father hoisted his wineglass. "A toast to the cook." He fixed a look on Nicky. "You're right. She's a first-class chef. Your mother and I will have to talk this over."

"Talk what over?" Natalie asked.

"Your future, Nattie."

Natalie rolled her eyes.

"Have you done any of the reading?" her mother asked.

"Some. I couldn't tell you what, though." Natalie sounded bored. "I'm thinking about getting a job at a restaurant in town."

Her parents exchanged looks but said nothing. Later they told Nicky they liked Dan and asked if she was serious about him. Nicky stared at them with disbelief before saying, "It's he and Natalie who are interested in each other, not me."

Her mother frowned. "He's too old for her."

When they left and Natalie and Dan disappeared, Nicky climbed into bed, although darkness had just set in. She didn't know why she was so worn out. Most nights she read herself to sleep with the windows open and a summer breeze wafting through the room. She jumped when Meg spoke from the open doorway.

Leaning against the door frame, half smiling, Meg

apologized. "Sorry, I didn't mean to startle you. I need someplace to sleep tonight."

"The sheets and stuff are in the closet next to the john."

Meg straightened and came into the room to sit on the edge of the bed. "How come you're between the sheets already? You have a rough day with your folks?"

Feeling naked because she wore only a thin white undershirt, Nicky pulled the sheet over her breasts. "Nothing better to do."

"You lonesome?" Meg raised blonde eyebrows.

Nicky knew she should say no. Instead, she told Meg about Margo and the Art Barn.

"Tough. I really am sorry. That's a rotten break," Meg said. "I'm glad I'm here. You shouldn't be alone."

"Oh, I'll be all right. Is Denise out of town?"

Meg grinned wickedly. "No, I'm at my folks." She moved closer to Nicky.

Wondering what Meg had in mind, Nicky licked her lips nervously. No one had come on to her for a long time. She wasn't even sure that Meg was being more than friendly.

"Natalie out with Dan?" Then, after Nicky nodded, "Want to play a game of cribbage?"

"Sure," Nicky said. She and Beth kept track of their games, and the board and cards were on the bedside table. "Should we play in the other room? Natalie might come home."

"So? Is it a crime to play a game of cribbage?" Meg glanced at the open doorway. "Want me to shut the door?"

"No."

Meg sat cross-legged on the bed while they played. They were in the middle of the tie-breaking third game when Natalie came in the back door and went up to her room. "Now we're really alone," Meg said. Looking directly into Nicky's eyes, she suggested casually, "Why don't I sleep here with you?"

Nicky was thinking that Meg's eyes looked like smoke. And when Meg's question registered, she felt a hot spurt of adrenalin. Shaking her head, she said almost angrily, "You know I'm involved, and you're in a relationship. What about Denise?"

"No one needs to know."

"I'd know." But she was focused on Meg's mouth, on the pulse beating in her throat. She saw Meg's slow smile and felt the flush on her skin deepen.

Still smiling, Meg got up. "I only wanted to share the bed. I didn't intend to take advantage of you." She laughed softly. "Sweet dreams."

Turning her light out, Nicky slipped under the sheet where she lay listening to Meg readying the couch. She refused even to consider where she and Meg might be heading.

VI

It had been years since Nicky had doubted herself, her future, her own worth. The first anxiety attack occurred while she was driving. With her heart pounding and her breath coming in rapid and shallow gasps, she pulled over to the side of the road to wait for the uncontrollable panic to subside. At first she was frightened but after a week of panicky episodes, she learned to wait them out.

She put a resume together and took it to a print shop, but thought it pitifully inadequate. All those years, after leaving UW Madison spent framing pictures at the Art Barn, selling a few of her own along the way . . . How could she have been so complacent? Why hadn't she prepared for job loss?

The Art Barn gave off an ambiance of failure. Fewer people came to its doors. The framing orders that had kept Nicky so busy tapered off to a few a week. She knew Margo would have to let her go before the sale of the building.

Poring over the classifieds every night, she saw no jobs which interested her or for which she qualified. She still had told no one except Beth and Meg about her dilemma. As the end of July neared, her panic grew. The monthly bills would come due. She hoped Meg would not be late with Brittle's board.

Meg's casual attitude toward her financial obligations irked Nicky, even though she thought it was unintentional. Annoyed that money had become so important, she resented the developing obsession with who owed her what. She lay in bed night after night, trying to figure out how she was going to pay the bills, adding up income against debt.

On the last Friday in July, when Margo stood hesitantly inside the doorway of the back room, Nicky tried to make it easier for her and spoke the words she thought Margo couldn't bring herself to say. "I'll just finish these. I won't take any more orders."

"We need to move the art I'm going to exhibit at home," Margo said.

"Why don't we do it Saturday," Nicky suggested. "I won't take money to move a friend, you know."

Shrugging, Margo said in a subdued voice, "I'll get a commission on your prints that sell. You realize that, don't you?"

Grateful for the "when" and not "if," Nicky only

smiled and continued working. She had considered framing on her own, but she would have to stock materials, and the farm wasn't easily accessible to the public. Few customers would drive ten miles out of town on the back roads just to get something framed. She couldn't afford the slim chance of success. You can't gamble with money you don't have, she told herself.

Margo's home, located near the lake, was large and too modern for Nicky's taste. It was, however, ideal as a gallery. Natural light filtered down through windows set just below the roof line in the long main room where Margo planned to display the pieces she thought would sell. Because the house stood outside the city limits, there were no restrictive zoning laws.

When they finished hanging the art, Nicky and Margo stepped back from the white walls and examined their work. Nicky sat on one of the leather couches placed back to back in the center of the room, and Margo plopped down next to her.

"God, it feels good to sit down, doesn't it? What do you think?" Margo waved an encompassing hand.

Nicky replied, "I'd buy, if I had any money." She shot a glance at Margo's stricken face and apologized. "I'm such an asshole. I'm sorry, Margo. I didn't mean anything."

"It's okay. You have a right to be angry. I feel so rotten about this."

Patting Margo's ring-laden hand, Nicky envied the large diamonds — not for themselves but for what they would bring. The proceeds from just one of those rings would keep her going for months. But then again, if she asked him, her dad would support her for a few months, too. That was what she didn't want, she reminded herself. She had to make it on her own.

"Margo, you can't keep the place open just for me. Any business has to make a profit, has to justify itself." She grinned. "Just write me a good reference."

Margo squeezed her hand, and the rings dug in painfully. "I'll sing your praises," she promised.

Met by Scrappy, Nicky walked to the fence and watched Tater gallop toward her across the pasture. On the days of weekend shows, he whinnied long after Brittle's answering calls from the trailer were carried beyond hearing. Wishing her life was so uncomplicated, she reached out to stroke his long, bony face, then snatched her fingers away when he nibbled at them. Meg said he did this because someone had once hand-fed him and he was looking for food. She decided to go shower and change.

There were still several hours of daylight left. With camera in hand, she started down the road with the dog. She found herself hesitating to take pictures. She couldn't develop color film herself. She'd have to pay to have it done. And, of course, there was the cost of new film to replace the used. Never before had she weighed the price of a photograph.

When she reached Dan's farm, she noticed the silver car parked down by the crossroads. She stopped in her tracks, then cautiously continued her walk. Along the way she pretended to photograph the cows in the field, the dog running ahead of her, the flowers blooming in the ditch. She got within a few hundred feet of the car before it drove off along the crossroad. Through her camera lens, she saw that it was as she'd thought, a Toyota Celica GT, but because the roadside grass had grown so high, she couldn't read the license plate.

She would have sworn that a woman was driving and wondered why the car was there when Beth wasn't around — although Beth *had* been at the farm that morning with Matt, when Nicky was helping Margo.

Nicky turned toward home. Meg and Natalie and Dan would probably be late. They usually stopped to eat after the show. On show days Dan asked his widowed father, who lived close by, to milk the cows. She decided to eat a sandwich and go to bed.

Startled awake by Scrappy's sharp bark, his toenails scrabbling for purchase as he dashed from the room, Nicky heard Natalie and Meg enter the house. She turned over and drifted back into a dream. Then, sensing someone in the bedroom, she snapped awake. Rolling onto her back, she recognized Meg standing next to the bed and muttered, "Why are you so late? Did you have truck trouble?"

"I'm glad you're awake." The edge of the bed sagged under Meg's weight.

"I'm only awake because you woke me up." Nicky switched on the bedside lamp.

"You should have been there to take pictures." Meg grinned, her teeth white against her tan face. "I was high point amateur. This was a Quarter Horse show. Do you know how tough it is to show Quarter Horse and do any good?"

"No," Nicky admitted, propping herself up on

pillows. She felt too vulnerable lying down. "I couldn't go." She had, for economy's sake, temporarily abandoned her planned series of horse show photographs.

"Here." Meg reached into her jeans pocket and dumped a pile of money on the bed. "Sorry it's late."

Nicky picked up the bills and straightened them, unable to quell the urge to count them. "There's a hundred and five dollars here." Nicky held out the extra five.

"You keep it. Consider it a late fee. They paid five dollars a point. Not bad, huh?" She laughed happily. "I filled Dan's truck and bought us all dinner. I want to celebrate." She stretched out on the bed next to Nicky as if that was where she belonged.

"Congratulations," Nicky said, then added, "You smell like Brittle."

"I'll take a shower and be back. Okay?"

"No, it's not okay. Sleep on the couch if you want."

When she next opened her eyes, it was because Meg was kissing her. "What the hell are you doing?"

"What I wanted to do ever since I first saw you at that gas station." Meg brushed her soft lips over Nicky's face, creating tantalizing chills of pleasure.

"You shouldn't be doing this," Nicky said, twisting in Meg's arms.

Starting in one corner, Meg slowly kissed the length of Nicky's mouth. "I know."

Reluctantly, hesitantly, Nicky parted her lips. Then she remembered. "The door . . ."

"It's shut," Meg said, breathing the words into her mouth.

As Meg cupped her breast, Nicky thought that

was where Beth's hand belonged. She asked, "Have you noticed that car parked down by the crossroads west of here?"

"What? No."

"It's a Toyota Celica. It was there today with a woman in it." Nicky was puzzled by that woman. She had expected the dangerous client to be a man.

Meg's hand stopped in mid-caress. She released Nicky and backed out of bed. "You've seen this car before?"

As she watched Meg pick up her clothes and start pulling them on, she wasn't sure whether she felt relief or disappointment or maybe a mixture of both with some guilt thrown in. Meg's body was shaped like an hourglass, with high, firm breasts, a flat belly, long muscular thighs. "Yes. It's often there when Beth's here and follows her when she leaves."

"Why do you think this person's after Beth?"

"I don't know. I thought it might be one of her clients, like in that awful movie *Cape Fear.*" She put her hands behind her head. "Where are you going?"

"Home. Maybe I'll see you tomorrow if I'm still alive."

"I hope so."

"Make sure Dan and Nattie take care of Brittle. Sorry about this."

A bit melodramatic, Nicky thought. She fell asleep with her hand between her legs. Once she had thought masturbation a wonderful release. Now it bored her.

Beth's arrival the next morning brought Nicky back to reality. Knowing that Meg was interested in her and that she had nearly succumbed to that interest made her less demanding, less angry. She was glad that Meg had not shown up yet. She needed time alone with Beth. Meg's parting words, she thought, were probably as unreliable as Meg herself.

Discovering that lovemaking kept her anxieties at bay, Nicky prolonged it for as long as she could. That afternoon, gratified by a surfeit of sex, she and Beth sunbathed on a blanket in the front yard. But Nicky could not chase worry away for long. "I have to go to the unemployment office tomorrow and file."

Beth lay belly down next to her, her face resting on her arms. "Have you sent out any resumes?"

"About fifty." It was more than a slight exaggeration. She could smell the coconut in the suntan lotion Beth was using. Her heart began its panicky beat. "Haven't heard a word from any of them."

"Well, give it a little time."

"I got a book from the library about interviews. If they ask me any of those stupid questions, I'll laugh."

"That'll get you hired," Beth remarked sarcastically.

She told Beth about Natalie and Dan and the restaurant idea. "Mom's in a frenzy. She claims Dan's too old for Nattie, but I think if he was a doctor, she wouldn't care about the nine years between them. She has preconceived notions of farmers. She doesn't want Nattie to spend her life raising hordes of children, milking cows and collecting eggs."

"Come on, Nicky. Doesn't your mother belong to the League of Women Voters and work for pro-choice groups? I thought she was a flaming liberal."

"She's still a snob, though, about her family.

She'll fight for the underdog, but she doesn't necessarily want her daughter to marry one."

The phone rang and Nicky raced inside, catching it before the answering machine clicked on. It was her mother.

"Is Natalie around, dear?"

"No, Mom." She had gone off with Dan earlier in the day.

"Did she tell you that we suggested she get a degree in restaurant management?"

"She told me she wanted to stay here."

"And take courses at the Tech." Her mother sounded resigned. "Well, tell her we'll talk to her soon."

"I will. You okay, Mom?"

"Busy. How's work?"

"All right." Nicky flushed at the lie. Sooner or later her parents would find out the Art Barn was closing its doors.

As Nicky hung up, Beth came inside to change. When Beth dropped her swimsuit, Nicky pounced on her and pushed her backwards onto the bed. She buried her face in Beth's neck, inhaling the suntan lotion. "You smell like summer."

Beth wrapped her arms and legs around Nicky. Tasting Beth's nipples, salty with sweat, Nicky emitted a low, lustful growl.

"Where's Meg?" Beth buried her fingers in Nicky's dark hair.

The question gave Nicky pause to remember her guilt. She lifted her head from between Beth's breasts. "It's not my day to watch her." Then, starting to work her way down Beth's body, she said, "I love sweaty women."

"I've got one more question before I surrender. Have you told your parents about the Art Barn being sold?" She tugged at Nicky's hair, forcing her head up.

"No," she replied after a brief pause. "I don't want to disappoint them. I don't want them to offer me money. I don't want their disapproval. I don't want them to know. Pick one or all of the above." She lowered her head again, determined not to lose her focus.

Beth pulled her closer and peeled off her suit. "You'd think we'd had enough sex for one day."

"I'll never get enough," she murmured, as she settled on top of Beth. They were a perfect fit, she thought. When their breasts met, so did their bellies and their mouths. She nibbled Beth's lips, then kissed her. "You taste like an orange." Beginning a slow pelvic thrust, she felt Beth move with her.

"Spread yourself," she whispered and shifted her weight. Her fingers slid gently over the taut, sensitive skin. She heard Beth's sharp intake of breath, felt her quiver under her touch. Her excitement fed her own.

After a few moments, Beth turned onto her side. "You spread yourself," she said thickly and reversed herself so that they were heads to tails.

Rolling, first one on top, then the other, they used their tongues and fingers to elicit an ecstasy that only came with practice and familiarity. As they surged toward climax, she thought there was nothing quite like this. It took her to another level where thought merged into sensation and pleasure overrode reason. She couldn't have stopped their headlong rush toward orgasm had her mother walked into the room.

* * * * *

Beth left around ten that night. Nicky was sitting in the dark on the front porch, one hand resting on Scrappy, when Natalie came in a half-hour later and found her there. "Mom called this afternoon, wanting to talk to you," Nicky said, looking at the shadow of her younger sister.

"She's afraid I'll marry Dan."

"Is that a possibility?"

"Maybe sometime. I'd live with him first. Do you mind my staying here and going to the Tech this fall?" Natalie sat down.

Smiling, Nicky teased, "Not as long as you cook for me."

"You're my guinea pig. Why are you sitting out here in the dark?"

"Thinking."

"Something's wrong, isn't it?"

Nicky felt Natalie's eyes on her. "Nope. Everything's hunky-dory," she lied, wondering why she always tried to hide her own failures from her family — even the small ones, even the ones that were not her fault — never giving them the chance to be a source of strength for her.

VII

Nicky delayed going to the employment opportunities office until midmorning on Monday. Natalie was making bread and watching the clock, while Nicky sat at the kitchen table in a splash of sunlight with a magazine spread in front of her and a cup of coffee cooling next to it. An August breeze through open windows mingled the scent of yeast with that of the roses growing along the edge of the garden. She wondered if the importance of life could be boiled down to a few moments of sensuous pleasure — minds meeting during a moment of passion, a photograph so piercingly clear as to be brilliant, a breathtaking view, a meaningful exchange of confidences, an odor that defined the season and embodied good memories.

"Are you expecting someone?" she finally asked, as Natalie shot another glance at the clock on the stove. Did Dan usually come over after milking? The look of annoyance on Natalie's face prompted her to say, "All right, I'm going."

After a quick shower, she gathered her purse and went out the door to the truck. Thinking that she had touched bottom, Nicky parked outside the unemployment compensation office on Monroe Street. For a few moments, she eyed the activity in the parking lot. Then, drawing a deep breath, she stepped out of the truck. Inside, block walls supported shelves on which people filled out pink forms and fingered worn telephone books. She felt as bleak as the building looked. A line of rather grim-faced men and women shuffled toward a single opening behind a counter.

In an adjoining room a TV offered video instructions to empty chairs. Nicky sat in one and listened to parts A and B of the video. She filled out a pink form and stood in line between two people who apparently knew each other. They talked around her until she changed places with the one in front of her. Fishing her social security card out of her purse, she studied faces to see how she fit in. The variety of age, shape, dress and hair dismayed her.

Forty minutes later, she reached the window and met the nut-brown gaze of the tall, thin woman on the other side of the counter. Nicky handed over the pink form and read the name plate: D. Carpenter.

The woman looked like she had sharp edges. Her brown frizzy hair gave her a startled appearance.

"How long does it usually take to get benefits?" Nicky added, "This is my first time here."

The woman's eyes darted down the form. "Well, first you'll get a claim card in the mail to fill out and send in. Maybe two weeks, if all goes well and you qualify. Sign here." She handed Nicky a booklet on filing for unemployment compensation. "Read this. It'll tell you all about it." Smiling, showing long white teeth, she said, "Good luck."

Nicky crossed the hall to the door marked Job Service Division, the state employment agency, where she read the notices on the bulletin board, filled out an employment application form and waited in line nearly an hour to talk to an agent.

A plump, pleasant-faced lady took the application form from her and offered her a chair, then studied Nicky's qualifications. "You're a photographer?" She appraised Nicky from behind wire-rimmed glasses. Her glossy red lips and rouge-brightened cheeks gave her a cheerful, clown-like appearance. "And you've worked in retail?" She took in Nicky's nod and glanced down again. "You frame pictures?"

"Yes." Nicky explained, "I'm a photographer, I do framing, I develop black-and-white film. I worked in an art gallery." She supposed that could be construed as retail.

"When something comes up, we'll call or send you a card," the woman told her. "I don't have anything now, but jobs in retail open up all the time."

Nicky had a sneaking suspicion she wouldn't be

allowed to refuse a job and still collect unemployment benefits, which meant she could end up selling lingerie at Dayton's. She shivered at the thought.

Out the door with the rest of the day in front of her, gulping in the fresh air, she drove around for a while before realizing that she was needlessly burning gasoline. Was that how she was going to spend her life now, she wondered, worrying about the cost of every move she made, everything she did?

Driving toward the farm, it occurred to her that now she had time to make some improvements. The barn needed scraping and painting. But the problem was she didn't feel like doing anything, and when she got home around four, she entered the barn instead of the house. Climbing the stacked bales in the hayloft, she worked her way to the rectangular opening at the far end and pushed the wooden shutters open.

Shafts of sunlight poured in, streaking the hay with dusty brightness. The countryside spread out below — rectangular fields of crops and cattle, the lines of roads, houses and barns laid out in patterns. A John Deere tractor worked its way up and down a field of alfalfa, cutting hay with a mower which then fed the clippings into a gravity feed wagon. She assumed Dan was in the enclosed cab of the large John Deere, probably with Natalie at his side, since the tractor was on his property. It made her lonesome.

She fell asleep in the blanket of sunshine and didn't awaken until the sun had slipped far to the west. She found Natalie and Dan in the kitchen.

Lifting the lid on a large pot of steaming corn on the cob, she said approvingly, "Looks good. I'm ravenous."

"You're not working, are you?" Natalie asked, regarding her with a level gaze, her arms folded.

Nicky paused with the lid in hand, steam burning her arm. "I told you, I went in late today."

"You came home early, too," Natalie pointed out.

Irritated by the burn and the confrontation, she slammed the lid on the pot and turned cold water on her arm. "Okay, you're right. Margo had to close the Art Barn. If you tell Mom and Dad, I'll be real hard to live with, Nattie."

"Why would I tell them? I don't tell them anything else. Where've you been all day?"

Nicky sat at the table with Dan. "At the unemployment office, Job Services, the barn. Nice view from the loft."

"I could use help," Dan said quietly.

Scoffing softly, she turned toward him. "Thanks, Dan, but it's tough enough for a farmer to make a living these days." She knew that farming was immensely productive and just as unrewarded. "I'll help you, but not for money. You always help me when I need you," she added with a shrug.

"I've got a contract with the county for mowing roadsides, and I haven't had time to get in a second cutting. They pay me. I'll pay you some of it."

"What about Natalie here? She'd look good on a tractor."

"Yeah, what about me?" Natalie asked indignantly, fishing the corn out of the pot and setting the bowl down hard. Two cobs jumped out onto the table. "Why didn't you suggest that to me?"

"I didn't think of it," Dan said. "Look. I don't care who does it, just so it gets done."

"Sorry," Nicky whispered when Natalie turned back to the stove.

Nicky awakened to rain on Friday. She was disturbed because Beth, who normally called every day, hadn't talked to her yesterday. Granted, she had been cutting roadsides for Dan since Wednesday, and she hadn't been home during the daylight hours, nor had she herself made any attempt to contact Beth. She also realized that she hadn't seen Meg since Saturday and wondered if she was avoiding her.

It would be a good day to drive to the *Fox Cities Gazette* office, she thought, to inquire about her cover letter and resume and ask for an interview. She had tried to do that on Tuesday and had been unable to force herself to get out of the truck.

Scrappy whined from next to the bed, and Nicky rolled onto her side. She listened for other sounds in the house and heard rain hitting the distant roof, spattering the windows. "Gotta go outside, little buddy?" But when she opened the door for him, he wouldn't leave the house. The ringing phone pulled her away from the back door.

"I've been calling since Wednesday. I was ready to send out the rescue squad," Beth said, her voice tinged with desperation.

"I've been on a tractor, mowing roadsides for Dan." She scratched at her arm. "Except for the poison ivy, it's not a bad way to make a buck — lots of sunshine and fresh air and time to think." She could almost smell the hot, rank mixture of weeds and diesel fumes.

Beth's voice dropped so low that Nicky strained to hear her. "I know it's as much my fault as yours, but we never should have sent each other cards."

Alarmed, Nicky's heart tripped into overtime. She tried to recall her last card, how incriminating it might have been. She sometimes scribbled torrid references to their love life. Damn it. Why hadn't she recognized the danger of putting such feelings on paper? "Why?" she whispered.

"Mark found the one you sent last week. He's up in arms. I never saw this side of him."

"Where are you?" What exactly had it said? For the life of her, she couldn't remember. She had sent the card on impulse, because she had thought it funny and appropriate, and added a few words of her own.

"On a pay phone at the health club."

"What happened? What did he say?"

Beth's voice shook slightly, which frightened Nicky even more because Beth always seemed so in control. "He wants me to move the pony to another stable. He doesn't want me to see you anymore."

Nicky's heart, thumping in her throat, impeded her breathing. She looked toward the ceiling and blinked back tears. "Are you going to go along with him?" There was a long pause. She kicked the floorboard savagely. "Are you?"

"I think we should lay low for a while."

"Meaning I won't see you? What about Tater?"

"Just leave him there for now. I'll work on Mark.

I won't see you this weekend, I know that. I'll call you whenever I can."

Nicky slammed the receiver into its cradle. "Fuck, fuck, fuck," she said, throwing herself into the nearest chair.

Scrappy tucked tail and retreated to a far corner of the room, where he curled up in an untidy heap. He eyed her reproachfully, his sorrowful gaze screened behind tangled brows.

"Sorry," she said, and the black tail thumped briefly. Why was it you could always see so well what you shouldn't have done when it was too late to undo it? Well, she thought with a sigh, this would tell her how much Beth valued their relationship. Maybe Mark would recognize Nicky's place in Beth's life. Ha, fat chance.

Somehow, she had to force herself out of the chair and into the shower. She needed to make a real effort to find a job, especially now that she might lose Tater's board.

Sitting in her truck outside the *Gazette* office building, the rain washing down her windshield, she wondered why it was so hard for her to just ask if her resume was being considered and if an interview could be scheduled. She had dressed in her only suit and brought her portfolio in hopes that she might see someone in personnel.

The receptionist greeted her with a smile and asked her to take a chair while she went to make inquiries. Nicky selected a dog-eared *People* magazine and paged through it. She looked up when the young woman returned, her brightly colored skirt swishing around admirably shaped legs. The girl looked no older than Natalie, yet Nicky envied her her job.

"They're in a meeting," the girl said.

Nicky thought the meeting was probably as phony as the receptionist's smile. "I don't mind waiting."

"Sure. I'll let Mr. Glaeser know that you're still here." She picked up a phone and spoke into it.

Absorbed in an article, Nicky didn't notice Mr. Glaeser until he spoke. She jumped at the sound of his voice, and the magazine fell to the floor as she quickly stood. Then she accidentally butted his shoulder as they both stooped to pick it up. She knew she had turned crimson. Her eyes felt like burnt holes in the flush of her skin. "Sorry," she stammered, watching him set the magazine on the end table.

"You're Nicole Hennessey? I'm Jim Glaeser." Offering her a limp handshake that contradicted his size, he looked down at her with an amused smile. "I'm sorry we haven't contacted you about your resume. We have no need for another photographer right now. But if you could send some samples of your work."

"I have some here." She handed him the portfolio.

"You came prepared," he said. "I like that. We'll certainly keep you in mind. In the meantime, if you take any newsworthy pictures, please send them. We pay for those."

Knowing she had been dismissed, she went out into the rain. Seated behind the steering wheel once again, she touched the dampness of her armpits and shrugged out of the suit jacket. A headache was working its way forward from the recesses of her brain. Her next scheduled stop was the photography studio on Main Street.

They didn't need a photographer either. The eager owner showed her around the studio, which made her realize how little she wanted to take portraits.

She decided she would rather mow roadsides. At least, there was an element of excitement in the endeavor. Every time she mowed a steep incline, her adrenaline kicked in. Driving a tractor was a dangerous occupation. Next week maybe she'd look at developing film for Photoplay.

The rain had stopped. Catching glimpses of blue sky and sun behind the shredded clouds, she rolled down the window. Steam rose from puddles on the pavement. Snatches of birdsong reached her ears as she picked up speed out of town.

After supper that evening, she watched Dan check the blades on the six-foot field mower mounted on the three-point hitch of the mowing tractor, a 275 Massey Ferguson. She had parked it in her barn on Thursday evening after filling it at his fuel tank. "They're good and sharp," he said.

Just then, she saw the Rabbit splash down the driveway. She hadn't seen Meg since she had backed out of her bed. There was someone else in the car with her, a woman who looked like the D. Carpenter from the unemployment agency. Nicky stared, her thought process working methodically. D could stand for Denise. Was it possible that Meg was living with the thin, frizzy-haired woman with nut-brown eyes — the woman with the jagged edges?

She watched with disbelief as the very same D.

Carpenter from the unemployment office got out of the VW. God, she thought, what a mismatched pair. She had imagined Denise to be handsome, charismatic. Who else could be expected to control an attractive, sexual woman like Meg?

Walking out of the barn with Dan and Natalie, she greeted Meg. When Denise pulled back in apparent alarm from Scrappy's rush and bark, Nicky apologized and took hold of his new red nylon collar.

Meg introduced them to Denise, who said about Nicky, "We met." She did not say where or how, which Nicky attributed to discretion.

Looking from Denise to Meg, Nicky strained for conversation. She didn't know whether she should ask about horse shows or Brittle, even though she was eager to go to the next show. She was willing to do anything to get Beth out of her mind. All day her heart had felt bruised and damaged, her stomach nauseated, her intestines twisted.

Natalie asked for her. "Showtime tomorrow?"

Meg glanced at Denise, who was still nervously eyeing the dog. "There's one Sunday. Want to go to a horse show?"

Denise's smile looked as fragile as she did. Her movements were quick and bird-like. "Sure. Where's the horse?"

"I'll have to come out tomorrow and get him ready," Meg said, taking Brittle out of his makeshift stall and turning him loose. He galloped across the wet pasture toward a snorting Tater. Meg nodded her head in their direction. "Is Matt coming out tomorrow?"

The physical pain caught Nicky off guard. She

didn't know her heart would ache again, as it had when Beth married Mark. She thought she was too old and too reasonable to feel crushed by Beth's decision to "lay low." Shaking her head, she forced a smile.

Meg departed with Denise, leaving Nicky alone with the dog. Natalie and Dan had already gone out for the evening. Nicky desperately needed to talk with Beth about Mark's finding the card and what that meant for herself and Beth. She wanted to tell her about Denise and Meg and discuss her job search. But there was no one to answer any of her questions or listen to her complaints. She realized that her relationship with Beth was unsatisfactory and that her life was empty.

When Meg arrived alone the next day, walking into the kitchen with only a knock and a yell to announce her presence, Nicky was already up. She put aside the morning paper and poured Meg some coffee.

"You remember telling me about the Toyota Celica parked down at the crossroads last Saturday?"

Nicky set the pot back under the coffee maker. "Let me guess," she said, suddenly seeing the light. "Denise was in that car. It wasn't someone watching Beth at all. She was watching you."

"Bingo," Meg said.

"Why do you put up with that shit?" she asked, unable to ask what she really wanted to know. There must be more to Denise than was readily apparent, something that drew Meg to her.

"I lied to her. She has a right to be angry."

"Granted, you shouldn't lie to her, but why do

you feel you have to? And she had no right to spy on you, anyway." Nicky sat across the table from Meg and looked into her gray eyes.

"I know all those things. I have no answers." She sighed heavily and changed the subject. "I've got a lot of work to do on that horse. Are you going with us tomorrow?" When Nicky nodded, she said, "Is Beth coming out?"

Nicky told her about Mark finding the card. "Beth thinks we shouldn't push seeing each other right now." She hadn't meant to say anything and listened with mild surprise to her own voice, toneless with depression.

"I thought something was wrong yesterday. You've got your own set of problems, woman." Meg reached across the table and took Nicky's hands. "Why don't you help me get Brittle ready to show? It'll take our minds off our troubles."

VIII

Nicky treated the horse show as more than a welcome diversion. She walked the show grounds taking pictures of little kids — leading fifteen-hand horses, riding in the walk-trot class — dressed in Western hats and chaps. She photographed some of the many dogs, adorned with brightly colored scarves, tied to horse trailers or wandering underfoot. She filmed the older kids working and showing their horses or just relaxing in the saddle talking to friends. And, of course, she focused on the other classes and the winners.

Nicky had ridden with Natalie and Dan in his truck, which towed the horse trailer. Denise and Meg had followed in the Volkswagen. Once there, though, Denise tagged along with Nicky, bending Nicky's ear with questions.

"I'm still learning horse photography," Nicky told her. She had learned to avoid certain angles, such as head-on shots that made a horse's head appear disproportionately large and its front end narrow.

Denise looked at the ground as she walked, occasionally glancing ahead or at Nicky. "I'd like to see your work."

"It's on exhibit at Phelan's Gallery on Park Drive near the lake." Nicky had talked with Margo that morning. Having sold two more of her photographs, Margo had asked Nicky to replace them with new ones. The horse art series had once again become a real possibility.

"Maybe you could sell some of these pictures you're taking here to the people who are in them — especially the ones of kids."

Nicky stared at Denise, wondering why she hadn't thought of that. A horse and rider trotted past, enclosing them in a swirl of dirt. Even as the dust settled, her thoughts moved ahead. She could talk to the show committees, maybe get permission to set up a booth at future shows. The thing was, she didn't have the equipment to develop color film.

"Nicky, I think we should get out of the road." Denise plucked her sleeve.

Dozens of horses were headed toward the show

ring. She realized it must be the break. She needed to set up her tripod for the afternoon classes.

On the way home, Nicky asked Natalie and Dan if they enjoyed the shows.

Dan said, "Well, I started going because Natalie wanted to. Now I guess we both go so that Meg can get Brittle there. It's okay." He paused and leaned forward to look past Natalie at Nicky. "You can pull my trailer with your truck any time you want. Brittle's doing too well to stop now."

"That's for sure. He's won every pleasure class I've seen," Natalie said. "Some guy asked Meg to put a price on him today. She wouldn't do it."

Staring out the window, Nicky hoped Denise had been with her, not Meg, when the offer was made. She sensed that Denise would sell Brittle cheap.

Rolling and grunting, Brittle coated himself with the soil of the barn lot. When Meg opened the gate, he dug in his hindquarters and propelled himself with his usual loud flatulence across the field. Tater, who had been snorting and prancing impatiently at the pasture gate, squealed and dashed in pursuit. Running after them, Scrappy returned moments later with a smug look, as if he had chased them off.

Nicky remarked wryly, "Brittle has no idea that he's such a star."

"He's the soul of modesty, isn't he?" Meg fished her winnings out of her pockets. "He's high-point amateur pleasure horse in the state already, and I think he may be high-point horse in Senior Western Pleasure too."

"That should make him worth big bucks, shouldn't it?" Denise asked.

The three of them hung on the fence, eyeing the galloping horses. Natalie and Dan had gone into the house.

"You going next weekend?" Meg asked Nicky, digging a hole with the toe of her Western boot, wisps of fair hair curling around her tanned face.

"Maybe I'll drive. Call me when you know who's putting on the next show."

"We're talking Saturday and Sunday and maybe Friday night."

Denise remained silent, her eyes darting from Meg to Nicky and back again. She seemed anxious to leave.

Nicky was loath to let them go, although she couldn't have said why. She and Meg had talked yesterday while Meg bathed and clipped Brittle. Nicky had held the lead rope, so distressed by her Friday phone conversation with Beth that she had been barely aware of the horse.

Feeling sorry for herself, she had said, "I won't know what to do with myself on weekends."

"I know what to do with you," Meg had replied. "Showtime."

The sun was setting, staining the sky with color which Nicky thought prophesied a nice Monday. She could mow for Dan. She was beginning to enjoy mowing, if only because it gave her a purpose.

She had to see that the horse show photographs were developed before next weekend, though. Waving at the Rabbit, she turned toward the house with Scrappy on her heels.

Inside, the answering machine registered zero. No messages. Her expectations dropped along with her heart. If Natalie's leftovers hadn't smelled so good, she would have foregone supper and gone to bed. Her sister regarded her questioningly as she entered the kitchen.

"Beth didn't come out this weekend. She all right?"

Nicky looked from Natalie to Dan and back again. Did they know enough about her life to suspect her distress? She was tired of hiding her feelings. Nevertheless, she passed a grimace off as a smile and said, "She had other things to do, I guess. Smells good."

As they sat down to eat, Natalie announced, "I'm going to be cutting veggies at The Goose Inn next week. I need some spending money."

Nicky felt abandoned.

Monday morning, Nicky took the film to Photoplay. Knowing she had to actively look for a job weekly in order to meet the requirements for continued unemployment benefits, she filled out an application.

By midmorning it was hot. She climbed onto the seat of Dan's Massey Ferguson. Shoving in the fuel knob, she turned the key and listened to the throbbing engine. This was power, she thought. Once the throttle was set and the transmission in gear, the tractor could only be stopped by shutting off its fuel supply or by something immovable. What gave it so much power was not the engine, but the low gears and large, deeply treaded rear tires.

She had put Scrappy inside the house so that he couldn't follow her. The rear-mounted mower, its heavy blades turning at high speed, chopped up saplings and bushes as if they were weeds. It had no respect for life.

Just before noon, she ran over the yellow-jacket hole. Weed seeds clung to her sweaty skin as she peered through pollen-colored sunglasses at the unmown grass next to her, trying to locate rocks and holes she needed to avoid on her next swipe. The first sting startled her. Glancing at her denim-clad legs, she saw an army of yellow jackets swarming upward. She had enough presence of mind to put the Massey into neutral before jumping off and running, screaming until she had swatted the last attacking insect from her body. Then she turned and stared at the bright red tractor as if it had somehow betrayed her. It vibrated to the beat of its diesel engine.

Standing at the edge of the blacktop, she wondered how she was going to manage a safe return to the Massey. Absently, she scratched at the many wasp stings on her legs and body. She didn't recognize Beth's Probe until it was nearly upon her.

"What are you doing?" Beth asked, parking next to her.

Although adrenaline no longer raced through her veins, Nicky breathed heavily. "I must've run over a nest of yellow jackets."

Elegantly clad in a linen suit and heels, Beth stepped out of her car. "Let me see."

Still scratching, Nicky said, "I'd have to take off my jeans."

"Then let's go back to the house and check you over."

"I can't leave the tractor running. And if I turn it off, I might get stung again." Still, she knew she had to approach the Massey sooner or later. With her heart in her throat, she pulled the shut-off knob, grabbed the key, and returned to Beth in a matter of seconds. She opened the passenger door of the Probe. "What are you doing out here?" Then hesitating, knowing that sweat had plastered weed seeds and a dusting of pollen to her skin, she inquired, "You sure you want me in your car?"

"Get in," Beth ordered. "Do you know if you're allergic?"

"I'd be dead if I were."

At the house, empty except for the two of them and the dog, Nicky turned on the shower and shed her clothes. The water felt wonderfully soothing as it coursed over her, momentarily taking the itch out of the swelling stings.

Beth sat on the toilet lid and talked to her. "It was a dreadful weekend. I expected Mark to be more reasonable, more tolerant. And if not that, then to tell me to leave. He did neither." Nicky heard her sigh over the torrent of water and thought she whispered, "He forced himself on me."

Shoving back the shower curtain, she asked, "He did what?"

"He wanted to know what we did, how often we did it, how long we've been doing it. When I wouldn't tell him, he told me I'd better never see you again or he'd see that I never saw Matt again. Now I know how my clients feel during interrogation." Beth looked up at her. "You'd think I'd be the last person he'd want to fuck."

Nicky was appalled. "He didn't mean that, did he? About Matt?"

Tears streaked Beth's face. Her voice caught on

her words, breaking the sentences into pieces. "He . . . can't do . . . that. He was . . . just so . . . angry."

"Where was Matt?"

"At a friend's." Beth sniffed and faced the mirror to repair her makeup. "That wasn't the worst, though." Her reflection met Nicky's. "He cried, finally, after the anger. That was the worst part."

Nicky stepped out onto a bath mat. "I nearly went crazy — not being able to talk to you, not knowing what was going on." She reached for a towel but Beth grabbed it first and rubbed her dry.

"You were right. I never should have married," she admitted, smearing cortisone cream on the welts covering Nicky. "You're a mess, sweetie."

"Thanks," Nicky said dryly, attempting to put her arms around Beth.

Beth shrugged away. "Let me put this stuff on you first. I can't stay long. He might come looking for me."

Terrific. Were they just to have a few snitched moments now? She said, "I was frantic. If I hadn't had Meg to talk to on Saturday, I might have lost it." The anxiety attacks were worsening and increasing, but she didn't tell that to Beth either. Instead, she told her about Denise.

But Beth, preoccupied and withdrawn, left as soon as Nicky was dressed, giving her a quick hug and kiss. When Nicky questioned where and when they would next meet, she said, "I'll call you."

After dinner that night, Dan drove with Nicky to the stranded tractor. He told her that yellow jackets, known for their aggressive behavior, retired to their ground holes after dark. Pouring gasoline down the small hole, he said, "Sorry you had to get stung.

They're nasty little buggers, but this bunch won't bother you anymore."

While she watched him immolate the nest, she wondered how such tiny creatures could frighten her half out of her wits. She decided that she had to look harder for a real job.

The next morning Meg knocked on the back door and opened it, calling, "Hello." She smiled at Nicky. "What happened to you?"

"Mowing wasps." Nicky got up from the table to pour Meg a cup of coffee. "I'm taking a day off. How about you? Why are you here?"

"I'm taking a day off too. I hoped you'd be home." She sat down with a grunt. "How's it going, anyway."

"I've been better." No job, no money, no lover, she thought. What a pisser. Meeting Meg's gray-eyed gaze, she said, "How come you took a day off?"

"Have you been outside yet?" Nicky shook her head. "It's pretty."

"There've been lots of pretty days."

"I wanted to see you alone." She took a sip of coffee.

"You just saw me alone on Saturday." Nicky's pulse picked up speed. Denise would be at work today. There wouldn't be any chance of her dropping in. "Tell me about you and Denise, how you met."

Meg gave her another crooked smile. "Not now, Nicky."

Nicky's throat thickened. She swallowed coffee and choked on the hot, black liquid.

"Is Nattie at work?"

Nodding, Nicky found her voice and it sounded thin. "Beth came out yesterday."

Meg stood and stretched. "I don't want to talk about Beth either."

Distracted by the outline of Meg's body under her thin T-shirt, she asked, "What do you want to talk about?"

Easing into a relaxed position, she smiled at Nicky. "I don't want to talk."

Nicky's heart hammered erratically. She gripped her coffee cup with whitened fingers. She had known this moment was coming; she just hadn't known when or what she would do when it did. Noticing Meg's tongue dart over her lips, she licked her own.

Meg reached for Nicky's hand. "Come on." When Nicky shook her head, she said, "Please."

Sunlight covered the quilt on the bed, the braided rug on the wood floor. The whites, reds, greens, blues and browns looked bright and clean. Nicky felt as if she were in a dream. She told herself it wasn't too late to say no, but something inside her wanted to know what Meg would be like in bed. She remembered the preview.

Meg lifted Nicky's shirt off, then slid her shorts and panties down her legs and off her feet. She hurriedly removed her own clothes while Nicky sat naked on the bed.

The sun played over their bodies when they lay down together. With a fingertip Nicky traced the delicate blue veins showing through the pale skin of Meg's breasts. Meg's gray eyes, slightly hooded and dark with desire, kept track of her touch until she took Nicky's face between her hands and kissed her.

Their tongues laced and they reached between each other's legs. Nicky felt the ache of desire — familiar and exquisite — gather and grow with the rhythm of Meg's fingers. She surrendered to it. Unable to hold off climax, she moved with Meg's touch and increased the speed of her own. Hearing their ragged breathing and soft moans, she was unable to differentiate her sounds from Meg's.

After the passion, Nicky wondered about its intensity, its origin. They lay gulping air, steadying each other with an embrace. She was not prepared when Meg started to move down her body. Grasping her under the armpits, she met Meg's eyes. "No."

With raised eyebrows and a seductive smile, Meg replied, "Yes, I want to." And before Nicky could protest further, she turned around and twisted out of Nicky's grip.

Feeling the warm tongue, Nicky gasped and arched away from it. But in the ensuing moments, she felt herself quivering toward it. Finally, consumed with lust, she pulled Meg's hips downward to taste her.

As they lay under the cover of sun, their ardor fulfilled, Nicky felt shame. Beth cheated on her with Mark all the time, but this was the first time she had been unfaithful in return. She wasn't responsible for Meg's behavior, but was she herself just another in a long line of Meg's conquests? Fearing she'd been an easy lay, that she hadn't resisted enough, she said, "We shouldn't have done that."

"Why not?" Meg asked, kissing her on the mouth.

Nicky sniffed for her own scent and didn't find it. "You know why. I'm with Beth. You're with Denise."

"You can't even see Beth without sneaking around," Meg pointed out. "She's married."

Stung, Nicky shot back, "And you're controlled by Denise."

Meg let her go and rolled onto her back. She put her hands behind her head, her fair hair fanning out under and between her fingers. Lying on her side, Nicky attempted to keep her eyes off Meg's full breasts.

"You're right," Meg conceded. "I'm afraid of her mouth. When I met her, I'd just come out. She had a job. I didn't. She supported me through my last year of school." Meg turned her head and met Nicky's eyes. "I went to college late, after I'd been out of high school five years."

"You feel obligated to her?"

Meg shrugged tan shoulders. "I guess I do, and I know she loves me."

The bed was cooling beneath them without the heat of their desire and the warm sunlight. Nicky found the top sheet with her toes and pulled it up, then covered them both. She hated hiding Meg's breasts. "Do you do this often?"

Meg held Nicky's gaze. She looked serious. "I've done it a few times, yes. Denise isn't very sexual."

The back door slammed and Scrappy, who had been lying on the braided rug, leaped to his feet and scrambled out of the room. Nicky jumped from the bed and started for the bedroom door. "We better get dressed," she said in a low, panicky voice. "We don't need to get caught." She didn't pause to wonder whether anyone had the right to hold her actions against her. Reaching for the doorknob, she bumped into Natalie.

"Oh, I thought you must be sick or something," Natalie said, her dark blue eyes widening when she spied Meg. Her face reddened and she turned on her heel.

Nicky pulled on her clothes and chased after her. "Wait, Nattie," she called, but her sister was already out the back door and crossing the yard. Slumping against the kitchen doorframe, she felt defeated and fearful. This wasn't how she meant to come out to her family.

A few moments later, Meg emerged from the bedroom. She looked at Nicky and started to laugh. Hooting, she bent over and clasped her knees.

"I'm glad you find something funny about this. Maybe you'd like to share it with me?" Nicky said sarcastically.

Meg straightened. She began to say something but burst into more laughter.

In spite of herself, Nicky found herself responding. A small giggle escaped her.

Pointing a finger, Meg said, "Your clothes are on backwards and inside out."

"My mind is, too," Nicky remarked, looking down at herself. "What the hell am I going to say to Natalie? What if she tells my mother?"

Still smiling, Meg shrugged. "Nattie's okay. She won't tell."

IX

She was actually more worried about how she would explain Meg to Nattie than whether Natalie would tell their mother. She took the Massey out of the barn and down the road. As she drove the tractor off the blacktop and into the ditch, she reached down and turned on the power take-off. The heavy blades vibrated, shaking the mower deck as they began whipping around.

A rabbit shot out of the undergrowth and bounded into a field of corn next to her. Knowing the lethal power of the mower blades, she kept an eye out for movement in the weeds alongside and in front of her. So far she had unintentionally mowed up a few rabbits and one possum. She'd had to finish off the mortally wounded possum with a large wrench out of the tool box — a mercy killing, which she refused to think about.

Bumblebees settled on the purple blossoms of tall thistles, even as the thick stalks fell under the front end of the tractor. The thistles struck her legs, piercing her jeans, leaving prickly chaff stuck to her clothes and ankles. She cringed and pulled her legs in close.

Eventually, the large bees lit in her hair. She felt two of them crawling across her scalp and frantically tried to dislodge them with gloved fingers. Before she succeeded, they each stung her once. When she turned the tractor toward home late in the day, the bee stings — at first numbing — had created itchy lumps.

Filling the Massey at Dan's fuel pump, she saw neither him nor Natalie. They weren't around the house either when she slammed the screen door and went straight to the shower without even checking the answering machine.

She left off wondering what she would say to Natalie and thought instead about Beth. Perhaps Beth would sneak out more often during the week for short visits, or maybe she would confront Mark with her need to see Nicky. Knowing that both were just wishful thinking, based on her inability to give up Beth, she glumly considered her miserable options.

Washing her sore scalp thoroughly and scrubbing off the residue of weeds and pollen, she stepped out of the tub and rubbed herself dry. Scrappy's bark told her someone was probably in the house. Since Meg's car had been gone when she returned from mowing, there was a good chance the someone was her little sister.

Turning when Nicky entered the kitchen on bare feet, Natalie said, "I don't want to talk about it. You want to fuck women, go ahead. I prefer men."

Startled, Nicky replied, "Tit for tat, huh?"

"I didn't say that. I just said I don't want to discuss what I saw." She looked angry. "But what about Beth?"

Surprised, Nicky asked, "What about Beth?" Then added, "We're best friends."

Nattie snorted derisively. "Sure. That's all the two of you do behind closed doors is chew the fat."

"I thought you didn't want to talk about it."

"I don't." She swung toward the stove. "Don't worry. I won't tell Mom and Dad or Nancy or Neil."

Nicky took a step toward her sister. "Why are you so upset?"

"I don't know. I think I knew. I just didn't think about it." Her voice rose in anger. "You're my sister, for Christ's sake, and I catch you in the sack with another woman who happens to be a friend of mine. And on top of it, you're in love with still another woman who is married and has a kid."

Nicky was dumbstruck. Was it all so obvious? And was it really as sordid as it sounded? There were no good explanations. They all sounded sleazy. She could say she was horny and that she couldn't have sex with Beth right now, that she and Beth had been lovers before Beth married, that Meg came on to her not the other way around. There were lots of reasons for her behavior, but none of them came across as honorable or even defensible. She shrugged and went outside with Scrappy. At least he accepted her as she was.

The evening had turned cool and she shivered under sweats and wet hair. Dan had just parked his truck out by the barn and was walking toward the house. He smiled at her, and she knew immediately that Natalie had told him what she had seen.

"Hey, Nicky, I got a check from the county. I can pay you," he called.

"Leave it in the kitchen," she replied, hurrying away. She couldn't face two disapproving people across the supper table.

But once she reached the barn, she didn't know where to go. Deciding that the horses weren't going to keep her out of her own field anymore, she grabbed her rod from the old milk room and walked through the dew-wet grass to the trout stream. The horse and pony raised their heads and looked at her disinterestedly, then continued their grazing.

The days ended more abruptly now, and it was nearly dark an hour later when Dan led Brittle to his stall and started his truck. Nicky put the rod away and went inside where she checked for messages. Denise had called, inviting her to dinner on Thursday. She smiled at the sound of Beth's voice, asking to meet her for lunch tomorrow at an out-of-town restaurant called The Hermitage. She left an affirmative message on Denise's answering machine.

There were two lights on in the house — the one over the stove and the night-light next to the bathroom mirror. With the dog at her heels, she wandered into the kitchen and stuck her head in the refrigerator. Taped to a casserole dish was a note: *Eat Me.* She put the food in the microwave and sat at the table in the dimly lighted room. Propped against the peppermill was a check from Dan with a message under it: *Spend Me.* Nicky smiled a little, realizing that neither Natalie nor Dan was as angry or disgusted with her as she had feared.

The Hermitage, located on the banks of the Fox River, was one of the few eating establishments that offered dining outside and a view of the water. Nicky had never understood why more restaurant owners didn't build or buy next to some of the many area lakes and rivers.

She found Beth seated on the screened-in deck, staring at the slowly flowing water. Noticing the dejected slope of her shoulders, her hopes sank. And when Beth looked up and smiled sadly, she became alarmed.

"Bad news?" she asked.

"No hello, how are you?" Beth's eyebrows arched.

"How much time have you got? An hour, an hour and a half, two hours?" She sat down and stared at Beth hungrily.

Beth sighed. "You're in a lovely mood." When Nicky only shrugged, she asked, "Aren't you glad to see me at all?"

"You know I am. Don't play word games."

"This is the best I can do right now, short of leaving. And if I leave, I give up my son — at least for now — and my job. That's what you need, isn't it — someone to support? Have you found a job?"

The awful choices offered Beth reduced Nicky's reply to a whisper. "No. How's Matt?"

"He knows something's wrong. He just doesn't know what." She rearranged her table setting.

The waitress took their orders, and Nicky asked as soon as she left, "What's it like at home?"

Beth began folding her placemat, ripping off little pieces of it. Her voice sounded thick and choked, but what bothered Nicky most was her quivering chin. "I never know when he's going to lose his temper. And he's so angry, I think, because he can't control my feelings. He can control everything else. He can make me stay, but he can't make me forget you, and he can't make me not want to be with you." The muscles in her jaws worked tensely. "He's always asking me if I've talked to you, if I've seen you." She looked at Nicky and blinked back tears. "How's it for you?"

Regretting her own anger, which paled under Beth's anguish, Nicky reached across the table and took Beth's hand. "Better than it is for you. Is Mark still . . ." She couldn't finish the question, not sure that she wanted to hear the answer.

Beth turned Nicky's hand over and held it between her own. Her black lashes and hazel eyes glistened. "You know, that was a bone of contention in our marriage from the beginning." She apparently took note of Nicky's expression and hastened to add, "Oh, not once you and I began again but before that. Now he's always after me. He thinks that's why I took up with you." She patted their clasped hands and said forlornly, "The thing is, I think he really does love me."

The waitress placed two bowls of broccoli soup

before them and refilled their coffee cups. They stopped talking until she left, when Nicky forced herself to ask, "Do you love him?"

"I hate hurting him. I do love him, though not the way I love you. He's a good man."

Nicky shook her head in violent disagreement. "A good man would want you to be happy. He wouldn't try to keep you with threats."

Beth smiled wryly. "Give him a little time. It's been a terrific shock."

They ate in relative silence, hurrying because Beth had only an hour to spare from work. Nicky choked on the food.

As they hugged in the parking lot, she said, "You know, Beth, this would be easier to do if I knew when I'd see you again."

"I don't know. I'll call you. Say hello to Meg and Natalie," Beth said as she lowered herself into the Probe.

A stab of guilt brought a flush to Nicky's face, and she turned away.

On Thursday evening when Meg opened her apartment door, she carried a large, woolly gray cat which stared at Nicky out of enormous gray-green eyes. "Nicky, meet Figaro," she said, grinning mischievously, then whispered, "Don't tell Denise I played hooky Tuesday."

Was it only two days ago? It seemed much longer, but she had no intention of telling Denise anything. She was nervous just being here after their romp in the bed. She hadn't begged out of the invitation to forestall suspicion and to escape Natalie and Dan.

Figaro leaped to the carpet and stalked off with tail high. Meg said, "He doesn't know he's a huge hairball. He thinks he's a prince." She smiled radiantly. "Denise is in the kitchen, putting together an Italian banquet. Come on, let's get a beer to go with the lasagna."

Nicky followed her through an immaculate living room into a warm kitchen and greeted Denise, whose thin face was flushed with heat. "May I help?" she offered.

"You can keep me company. Meg, why don't you do the salad?"

Nicky looked around the kitchen, thinking it extraordinarily clean and uncluttered — like the living room, where there had been no magazines or books or newspapers lying around. Didn't they read? She sat at the table and Figaro jumped onto her lap, nearly causing her to drop her beer. "He doesn't feel like he's all hair," she remarked, watching him hunker down on her cotton slacks.

"Shove him off when you get tired of him," Meg advised. "By the way, I don't think I'm going to the Friday night show. I'll be out tomorrow to get Brittle ready for the weekend." She winked at Nicky, who frowned in an effort to discourage any flirting.

Denise turned from the pan where she was layering the ingredients. "Did you get the photos back from the Sunday show?"

"I'll pick them up tomorrow. I did talk to Saturday's show management. They said a professional photographer would add to the horse show.

They even have a table in one of the exhibit buildings reserved for me."

"I'll help if I can. I sure can't help Meg with the horse."

"That'd be great," Nicky said, feeling another pang of guilt. She vowed never to allow herself to be compromised by Meg again. Then she glanced at Meg and an unwelcome and unexpected spurt of excitement reminded her of the old saying, the one about "the spirit is willing but the flesh is weak."

Praising Denise's lasagna with the fervor of one who has transgressed and is trying to make amends, she ate twice as much as she wanted and felt bloated when she finally admitted she was full. "I need to walk a mile or two."

"Good idea," Meg agreed. "Let's just clean up this stuff and do that."

"I'll stay here. You two go. I've got work to do from my class."

"Denise is taking a women's creative writing class," Meg explained. "She writes some interesting stuff."

Denise beamed at the compliment.

Outside, in the early September evening — already dark and a little crisp — Meg hugged her lightweight jacket to her and leaned into the wind. "I like the feel of fall and I like you." She grinned.

"Don't wink at me around Denise or around anyone, for that matter. I felt like a scumbag in there. We can't do what we did again. You understand, Meg?" She thought she meant it.

Meg gave her a knowing smile. "Whatever you say."

"Let's hike a few blocks, and then I better go home."

On Friday, after mowing, she hooked up to Dan's stock trailer. He warned her, "Remember, give yourself plenty of time to stop. Don't crowd anyone. That's a lot of weight behind you." Dan studied the truck and trailer. "Brittle should have one of those fancy trailers."

"He's lucky you let him use this, or Meg's lucky, is more like it. You're good to us."

He smiled, his face ruddy from the sun and wind, his eyes squinting in the light. "Just be careful around corners and stopping and you'll be all right. And thanks for getting me off the hook. I've been away too many weekends."

Meg's Rabbit was parked in front of the barn when Nicky bounced down the driveway, the empty trailer clanging behind her. Scrappy barked alongside and looked chagrined when she got out of the truck. "Didn't know it was me, did you? Such a smart doggy." She bent to pat his black curls and briefly glimpsed his small, white teeth. "You have such a nice smile."

Standing on a wooden box, clipping Brittle's ears, Meg chewed her tongue in concentration. Horse hair rained around her. Tater, nickering for attention, pranced on the other side of the closed gate. Nicky stopped to wonder at the changes wrought in just a few months.

"I'm about done here. I'll wash him early tomorrow morning. Thanks for getting the trailer."

Nicky asked, "What time do you want to leave tomorrow?"

"Seven, eight o'clock." Meg gave her a warm smile. "Nattie invited me to dinner. Do you mind? Denise is meeting with her writers' group."

"Why should I mind?" she asked, knowing that she would feel awkward around Natalie with Meg there. "I have to get my photography stuff ready."

She set her camera with film, tripod, pads of receipts and order forms, a metal box with change, and the developed photographs near the back door. Then she allowed herself to look at the answering machine. She always felt slightly nauseated when there was a message from Beth, but she couldn't sit around the house waiting for her call, could she?

Beth's recorded words — "I'll be out Saturday afternoon around two. See you then." — filled her with despair. She couldn't even tell her that she would be gone, or where. Glancing at the clock, she took a chance and called the law firm and was rewarded with a taped reply. Banging down the receiver, she returned to the kitchen.

Natalie was busy at the stove, her back to the room. "Aren't you going to be gone tomorrow?"

"Yep. Will you be here?" Natalie looked slimmer, she thought, her dark hair falling in shiny curls to her shoulders.

"I've got to work tomorrow. Why don't you leave

a note on the back door for Beth and ask Dan to watch for her?"

Warming to her sister, Nicky thought it nice of her to care. "I'll do that." She waited for Natalie to turn around, suddenly wanting to see her face, to see if there were changes in it, too. "You asked Meg to dinner?"

Natalie's waves bobbed in a nod. She was all business at the stove, taking her cooking seriously. "Would you get me the soy sauce, please? And if you want, you can set the table."

Dinner was the usual good fare, although Natalie had less time to cook. The four of them were pleasantly relaxed with each other, but Nicky was too distracted about Beth's message to enjoy herself.

The next morning she taped a note to the back door before leaving with Meg and Denise. Quiet, making only necessary talk, they each sipped from cups of coffee. The truck windows were rolled down one-quarter of the way, and snatches of a meadowlark's song reached Nicky's ears. The cool freshness of morning drifted into the cab. By afternoon, at the horse show, Nicky knew, the air would be thick with dust and the ground hot and dry.

One of the fairground exhibit buildings was open for refreshments, and Denise helped her set up a photography display. Nicky had several photo enlargements from the last weekend's horse show to pin to the pegboard backdrop and an album of proofs to page through on the table provided. Denise offered to stay and handle any orders so that Nicky could roam the grounds with her camera.

Cleaning off her camera lens, Nicky glanced at her watch as Meg's Amateur Western Pleasure class entered the ring. It was four-fifteen. She figured Beth would have been here by now if she was going to come. Didn't Beth want to see her badly enough to drive the distance? Didn't she have enough spare time? Her guts twisted in the familiar knots brought on by these thoughts.

She had checked with Denise after every class throughout the day and found that, not only had she taken more than a dozen orders, there were people asking for posed portraits of their horses. So she had spent the greater part of her time taking shots of horses — either mounted or at halter, in the show ring and outside it — and made enough to at least pay her expenses. She thought it an immensely successful day, a new beginning of sorts and knew that she owed at least some of this success to Denise.

When they had loaded Brittle into the trailer, with his usual assortment of ribbons, and piled into the truck cab, they were tired, dirty and jubilant. As exultant as Nicky could be under the circumstances, she missed Beth and was inadvertently indebted to Denise. Did success always have a price?

Stopping on the way home, Nicky offered to buy dinner. An argument ensued over who owed what. Meg felt she should be doing the buying. Nicky had to agree with her but suggested a compromise. "You pay for the gas. I, at least, owe Denise a free meal."

All day she had been sitting on herself. Wanting to be home to see Beth, she knew she had to put that thought out of her mind. This had been an opportunity to make some bucks. She wasn't sure that she would skim much profit, after taking so many pictures of the same animals in different poses and then paying to have the film developed, but horse photography was still a learning process for her. She had decided to talk to someone at Photoplay, maybe work a deal with them.

And now, as they walked toward the truck-stop restaurant, she looked back with longing at the truck and trailer parked under a light, where they had left Brittle munching on hay. She wanted to jump in the cab and hurry home, just in case Beth was still waiting — although she knew the chance of that was so slim it was almost nonexistent.

Calling from a pay phone, she let the ringing continue until the machine came on and her own voice spoke in her ear. She listened to herself talk for a few seconds, still hoping someone would pick up the phone. In her mind's eye, she saw the interior of the old farmhouse with Scrappy probably sneaking a nap on the furniture — forbidden territory for him.

Meg looked up when she approached the booth. "Anyone home?"

She shook her head and slumped on the bench opposite Denise and Meg. Smiling a little, she asked, "You racked up another Amateur All-Around trophy today?" Meg ducked her head and grinned. "Modesty doesn't become you, Meg."

"He's just a great horse. It's not me — I know that."

"Denise, order the works. Would you like something to drink?"

"Vodka and tonic and a steak dinner," Denise said. "How does that sound? You know, they're supposed to have pretty good food here."

"I think we should all celebrate," Nicky said.

Before Meg climbed into the truck, she walked around the trailer to take a peek at Brittle. Denise and Nicky waited in the supercab. Night had fallen while they were in the restaurant, and a lot of the heat had escaped into the atmosphere. Nicky shivered at the sudden drop in temperature.

When Meg shrieked, Nicky was watching her through the side-view mirror. She was anxious to start home in case Beth had left a message. A chill of apprehension swept through her. "What is it?" she asked, jumping out of the truck, thinking perhaps something had happened to Brittle.

"He's gone!" Meg cried, running around the trailer and opening the tailgate. She searched the ditch, calling, "Brittle, Brittle."

They reached home around midnight, the three of them dog-tired and silent. The police had been called after everyone at the truck stop had searched in vain for the horse. Hoof prints had been found in the ditch nearby and along the shoulder of the road on the other side, where there were also tire tracks from a vehicle and trailer. The conclusion finally drawn was that the horse had been loaded into another trailer across the road and taken away. No one had seen anything.

Nicky remembered the first time she'd seen Brittle clamber into a trailer. He was so well-mannered, she thought, he'd do whatever was asked, he'd climb into any trailer.

She had no heart even for Beth's handwritten letter, left with Natalie. She stood holding it while they hashed over Brittle's disappearance with Dan and Natalie. They could hear Tater calling for his lost companion from the pasture gate. Nicky ached.

In bed, after a shower that failed to soothe her, she opened the envelope and read: *Nicky, my love, I understand your not being able to change your plans, because I know other people were involved. I didn't know I could get away until yesterday, and you couldn't have been more disappointed than I was today. So, you're filling your weekends now. I suppose that's good and I won't attempt to discourage you from doing whatever you need to do to get through this. I'll call you as soon as I can. Let's have lunch again at The Hermitage Monday. Love always, Beth.*

She fell asleep after reading the letter three times. In her dreams someone stole Scrappy and sold him for ten thousand dollars.

X

Sitting across the table from Beth, Nicky told her what had happened over the weekend.

Beth looked puzzled. "But why would anyone kidnap Brittle?"

Shrugging, hoping nothing terrible was happening to the horse, Nicky said, "Beats the hell out of me. Janet Larson — she's one of the horse show people — implied it might be to end his winning streak, but that seems a rather drastic solution." She had spent Sunday with Meg. They had gone to the horse show and spread the word that Brittle had been stolen. "Meg has his papers. She says he can't be shown or sold as a Quarter Horse without them." Nicky sighed, afraid to give voice to Meg's worse fear, in case saying it might make it happen, but she said it anyway. "Meg's afraid he'll be sold for meat."

"Horse meat is used to make dog food, you know." Beth stared at her in disbelief. "Well, now what?"

"Now we look for him, I guess. Meg was going to put some ads in newspapers and in the horse magazines. She was going to the sale barn." A chill crawled across her scalp and down her back. She changed the subject. "So how did you get away Saturday?" Her gaze traveled greedily over Beth's tanned face, paused at her lips, then followed the curve of her neck to her breasts, which were concealed by a tailored blouse. The need to do more than stare nearly overwhelmed her. She busied her hands with eating, forcing her attention elsewhere. "Was Mark out of town or something?"

"Yes," Beth admitted. "I brought Matt out to ride the pony, but I didn't know how to tack him up."

Throwing her napkin on the table, Nicky exploded, "Shit, Beth. Is anything ever going to change? Because I need to get on with my life." Surprised at her own outburst, she found herself panting from the unexpected anger. Did she really mean what she had just said? Probably not.

Looking around at the only other occupied table on the porch, Beth leaned forward. "No scenes, Nicky," she said firmly. Nicky knew how Beth hated calling attention to herself and thought she had gone into the wrong profession for her to be so self-conscious. "I'm doing the best I can. Be patient with me, please. And eat your food."

Nicky considered her spinach salad. It looked too good to waste. Putting her napkin back in her lap, she ate. "What about Tater?" The pony hadn't been ridden since Mark had found that unfortunate card. "He's lonesome. Maybe you should move him somewhere else." She wondered if everyone hurt themselves trying to inflict pain.

"I'll bring Matt out Friday after work. Could Meg be there? I've got the board money with me."

Nicky accepted the check. She needed it, after all. "I'll tell Meg."

When they said goodbye in the parking lot, Nicky said petulantly, "I'm horny. A little loving would be nice."

Beth held her in a hug and whispered in her ear, "I feel the same way. I'll look at my calendar. Maybe I can get away Wednesday at noon."

Nicky envisioned years of noon rendezvous once or twice a week. She was not overly enthused at the prospect.

"Tell Meg I'm sorry about Brittle." She peered at Nicky from the plush seat of the Probe.

Nicky climbed into her truck and drove home. She had stopped at Photoplay that morning with her rolls of negatives from the weekend shows. Tomorrow she would start working one day a week, receiving for her labor free developing services.

September sunshine differed from summer sunshine. It was mellower, as if its intensity had been burnt out, and it cast a soft, diffusive glow over the landscape. Flocking redwing blackbirds gathered shoulder to shoulder on telephone wires. Their calls reached her ears over the sound of the truck engine and the wind blowing through the open windows.

Changing clothes and shutting Scrappy in the house, Nicky drove the Massey out of the barn and was met by the sight of her mother's Volvo rocking toward her down the driveway. She pulled the fuel knob and coasted to a stop.

"What are you doing on that thing?" her mother asked, emerging from the driver's side.

It surprised Nicky to see her alone. "This is Dan's mowing tractor."

She took a step closer to where Nicky sat high off the ground. "Do you know how dangerous farm machinery is?"

"I'm careful, Mom."

"Is your sister in the house?"

Because of her part-time job at The Goose Inn and her full-time schedule at the Tech, Natalie was seldom home. At first Nicky had missed her presence — her tart tongue, her good cooking — but then she began to appreciate her own privacy again. When Nattie was home, Dan came around. The three of them ate together. "No. She's either at the Tech or at work."

Her mother frowned. "Well, get down off there and offer me some ice tea or something. It's not every day I come to visit."

Said just like a queen, Nicky reflected as she dutifully jumped to the ground and wiped her hands on her jeans. "Where have you been, anyway?"

"Busy." She looked and sounded annoyed. "Your sister, Nancy, needed someone to take care of the kids until she found somebody permanent, which she did last week. She started working in this travel agency, the one in the mall, you know." Nicky didn't know, but she listened as she hooked her arm through her mother's and walked toward the house. "Your brother moved out and I'm a bit lonesome."

"Sorry, Mom," she said, a little flattered.

"Well, I thought I'd see how things are going since I haven't heard from either one of you for such a long time. You could call, you know."

"So could you, Mom," Nicky replied, suddenly irritated.

Her mother sighed. "I can't stay long. Tell me, is Natalie still going out with that farmer?"

"Dan, you mean? He's a nice man — very helpful, kind, generous. He'd be a good catch." She wasn't sure if that was true and didn't know why she said it.

The dog leaped on them when Nicky opened the door. The last way she wanted to spend this afternoon was trapped inside. She poured them both a glass of ice tea and told her mother about Brittle. As she was reluctantly sitting down, Meg called.

"I can't work. I poked some poor guy at least four times before I got a vein. I thought he was going to pass out. I'm usually pretty good with a needle."

"My mother's here right now. Why don't you come out after work?"

When her mother left, Nicky drove the tractor to where she had stopped cutting last Friday. There were a few working hours before Meg showed up. Despite the pollen, thistles, poison ivy, stinging insects and occasional slaughter of small animals, mowing soothed her. It was a mindless, if sometimes destructive, embrace of the outdoors.

As she bounced along the rough roadside, she wondered what it was about her mother that sometimes bothered her so. Was it Cleo's classy good looks, which she had passed on only to Nancy? Did she envy her own mother? Was it because she so often felt as if she were her parents' last thought? She knew they loved her. That should be enough. Her father was always trying to foist money on her, his version of caring. Her mother gave advice and warnings as if they were gifts. And perhaps they were.

As she was going home, Meg passed her on the road, blowing her horn and waving. Nicky jerked at the unexpected sound, nearly sending the tractor into the ditch. When she turned off outside the barn and stiffly climbed down, she felt momentarily disoriented, overwhelmed by the relative quiet — birds singing, the dog barking, Tater whinnying.

She looked into Meg's gray eyes, at the whites streaked with red. "Haven't been sleeping much, have you? I have to take a quick shower."

Following her in, Meg said, "I keep seeing Brittle whenever I shut my eyes. I just want to know if he's all right."

Nicky closed the bathroom door and turned on the water, but Meg opened it and sat on the toilet seat. "It's not like I haven't seen you in the raw before, and I can't talk through a closed door."

"Wait till I get out. Beth might show up, or Natalie or Dan."

"I'll keep an eye out, and anyway, I can just tell

them I'm distraught or something, which is the truth."

Nicky shot her an exasperated look and stepped into the tub. So what if Beth found the two of them in the bathroom? So what if she found them in bed? But it did matter if Denise discovered them in a compromising position. She shuddered at the thought.

"I just hate Denise right now," Meg said. Nicky was startled. "She's so upset because I didn't sell Brittle before he disappeared. I have him insured for a bunch of money, but the insurance doesn't cover 'mysterious disappearance.' " Meg's voice faded to a murmur.

"What?" Nicky turned off the shower and grabbed a towel off the rack.

"She was counting on selling him for a down payment on a house. Can you believe it?" Meg's snort emphasized her incredulity. "What she doesn't know, and what you must never tell her, is that he's worth five times what she thinks he is." Meg's voice dropped again. "Some guy offered me twenty-five thousand for him at that last horse show."

Nicky nearly dropped the towel. "How did you latch onto this super-horse?"

"A friend gave him to me when he moved to California. He couldn't afford to take him. He taught me all I know about horses and showing." Her eyes lit up. "I love it, the showing part. When you're in a class and your horse is working good, you're on top of the world."

"And you think he'll be sold for meat when he's worth twenty-five-thousand dollars?" Nicky wrapped the towel around herself and went to her bedroom.

Meg was right behind her. "Like I said, he's not worth anything without his papers."

Nicky turned her back and pulled some clothes on over her still-damp skin.

"You have a cute butt."

"Quit looking." But Nicky was staring out the window. It had just occurred to her that if Brittle wasn't found there would be no more board money and maybe no more horse shows. Meg had been her door to a hoped-for career in horse photography — even though she had secretly denied such aspirations. Panic moved in and she attempted to ward it off with deep breaths.

"What's wrong, Nicky?"

"I have to call Margo." Why Margo came to mind, she didn't have a clue. She hadn't heard from her in weeks. Punching in Margo's number on the bedroom phone, listening to the rings, hearing Margo's voice on the machine and leaving her own message gave Nicky a chance to get a grip on her fear.

When she hung up, Meg said, "Let's go to the shows next weekend. I've got to keep looking for him, and you shouldn't stop the photography bit. You have picture orders, don't you?"

Nicky had been sitting on the edge of the bed. She smiled shakily at Meg, grateful for a thread of hope. That was when she realized how much she needed a plan, some kind of format for her future — and not just financial reassurance. More importantly, she couldn't drift through her days with nothing that needed to be done.

* * * * *

On Wednesday morning she awakened at six, tossed and turned until seven when she heard Nattie clatter down the stairs, and gave up on sleep. She mowed the yard and pasture, weeded the garden, cleaned the barn, and vacuumed the house. Preparing herself for Beth's arrival, she tried not to allow herself many expectations, but there was that hot rush of excitement when the Probe turned into the driveway.

Greeting Beth, she felt almost shy. "Have much trouble getting away?"

Unfolding herself from the car, Beth looked preoccupied. Then she gave Nicky a dazzling smile, as if putting away whatever was on her mind. "A piece of cake. I just had to lie to my secretary, plead a migraine, pretend a meeting with a client and sneak out of the office." She glanced up the drive and down the road and Nicky followed her gaze.

"Expecting someone?"

"I hope not."

"Want to come inside?"

"Why don't I change into some of your clothes and we'll go somewhere else?"

Nicky laid out a pair of jeans and T-shirt. She helped Beth out of her blouse and skirt, slip and camisole, and watched her peel off pantyhose. When Beth was down to bra and panties, Nicky took her hands and coaxed her onto the bed. "I can't wait."

Nicky closed her eyes and sighed with pleasure. This was the ultimate comfort: the warmth and softness of their bodies making contact. It was a brief thought before desire rolled over her.

With closed eyes she stroked Beth. She thought she knew the texture of her skin, the curves and planes, the intimate crevices. Exploring them all as if it were the first and last time, she was equally aware of Beth's hands and mouth on her. Neither could slow the rush of passion. Caressing, tasting, kissing — it was over quickly, almost before it began.

"Jesus," Beth breathed afterward. "Talk about suppressed desire." She raised herself on an elbow and peeked out the window. "Let's get cleaned up and dressed and go for a walk."

Reluctant to leave the bed, wanting to make love at a slower pace, Nicky responded only to Beth's apprehension. Pulling her close, she felt her tenseness and yielded to it. "Okay, Beth. Whatever you want."

Despite the brilliant day, there was an unmistakable feel of fall — the diminished heat of sun, a coolness to the air, the withering of grass. They strolled toward the stream. At first Tater had frightened them by bearing down on them at full gallop. But Nicky had clutched Beth's hand and stood her ground, unwilling to relinquish the field to him and knowing that he wouldn't hurt them, that he only wanted company. He trailed along behind them now, tossing his head at Scrappy's occasional lunges.

"He makes me nervous," Beth said.

"Meg said she'd be here Friday after work." She glanced at Beth. Wisps of hair curled damply against her neck. "Have you thought anymore about all of this?" she asked, wondering if the sex made her less desperate.

Beth sighed and turned to meet Nicky's gaze. Her pupils were black specks in the daylight, her hazel eyes the color of the stream — the color of fall, Nicky thought. "I've done nothing but think about it. My thoughts circle endlessly. Mark still isn't reasonable about any of this and he's always been a reasonable person. When I suggest a separation, he still threatens me with losing Matt and my job. I don't know what to do, Nicky."

"He knows he's got you by the short hairs," Nicky replied despairingly. She wouldn't suggest that Beth challenge him, because she knew that Beth must be more aware of her own options than she was. What drove her to distraction was that Beth let herself be controlled. She wished she hadn't marred the day by asking, but she had to know if there were any changes.

Beth looked at her watch. "I have to get back to the office soon."

When Nicky returned to the house, she found a message from Margo on the machine. She phoned her, and her voice made Nicky realize she missed working in the Art Barn, missed talking art with Margo.

"I've been out of town, Nicky. I didn't have time to call you before I left, but I sold two more prints. Have you got anymore, maybe some horse stuff?"

This small success swelled Nicky's self-esteem, which had shrunk dangerously in the last few days.

The next morning her spirits plummeted when she awakened to what looked like an all-day drizzle. Unable to stand being cooped up by the cold rain, not even with a book, she decided to check the job market.

Nicky had spent a day developing film at Photoplay. She wasn't sure that she wanted to spend every day of the week working there, but no one had offered her a full-time job or even remuneration for the work. She had two dozen rolls of film developed for free to take with her to the shows on the weekend.

Stopping in at Job Services, she talked to the lady with the red cheeks and ruby lips who cheerfully told her, "Sorry, honey, there're no openings. Maybe you want to expand your field of interest."

"I'll look harder," Nicky promised. She had been holding her own with the unemployment check, the board money and her share of the mowing profits, plus occasional infusions of monetary support from her dad for Natalie's board. Now she had lost the hundred dollars a month for Brittle, and soon the mowing would end.

She hadn't seen Denise since the weekend, and she crossed the hall to the unemployment division. It was hard to remain impartial toward Denise when Meg told all her faults.

Denise spotted her and waved her to the front of the line. Those waiting shuffled their feet disapprovingly and one man muttered, "Hey lady, the line starts at the rear."

"She's not in line," Denise said. "Are you? Want to go to lunch?"

Nicky glanced at her watch: eleven forty-five. She hadn't intended to spend the noon hour with Denise; she'd just planned to say hello. "When do you get off?"

"Let me get someone to take my place," Denise said, eliciting a collective moan from the people in line.

A dark-haired, heavy-set man took her window

and Denise went out into the cold rain with Nicky. She popped open her umbrella and walked toward the silver Celica. "Let's take my car."

This was the car Nicky had thought was being used to spy on Beth. That Denise had been watching Meg and Brittle instead was made more insidious now that Brittle was gone. Nicky shivered as she got into the car, escaping the wet chill.

When Denise turned the key, the windshield wipers quietly thumped across the glass. "Too bad we can't open the roof. I'm glad you stopped by. Where do you want to go for lunch?"

Nicky glanced at the moon roof over her head. "You decide." She wasn't even hungry.

The car shot out of the parking lot. Denise drove in spurts, a lot like the way she moved — slamming on the brakes at intersections, jerking forward and around corners, creeping in between. She jumped a lane and turned a corner without using her turn signal. It was almost more than Nicky could stand. Her teeth were clenched, her body rigid by the time they hit the curb outside Reynolds Restaurant. She caught herself breathing a sigh of relief and squelched it.

Over coffee and chili they discussed Brittle's disappearance and what it meant. "I know Meg is angry with me, but she can't really afford a horse. We'll never be able to buy a house as long as she has that horse, and she's gone every weekend. Before she started showing Brittle we used to spend our weekends together. We went places besides horse shows."

Nicky didn't know what to say, except what she was sure would be the wrong thing — that perhaps

Meg and Denise weren't compatible. "She's real worried about something bad happening to Brittle."

"I know. But it's hard to be sympathetic when she never worries about anything except that damn horse."

"There's good reason to worry, I think," Nicky said placatingly, spooning up the last of the chili, now thinking she could easily eat another bowl of it.

"The only good reason for finding him," Denise said darkly, "is to sell him, since she can't collect on his disappearance."

Momentarily speechless, Nicky stared at Denise. She had had a problem liking her from the beginning. This obvious disregard for what happened to Brittle didn't help. Floundering for less controversial conversation, she asked about work.

Distractedly running a hand over her hair, Denise said, "It's tiresome dealing with unhappy people all day long."

That night Nicky went to the livestock sale barn with Meg, who had come over after work and begged her to go. "I went Tuesday night alone. We don't have to sit through the entire auction, just see what horses they're selling. It'll take maybe an hour."

She told Meg about her lunch with Denise, but Meg said nothing, hardly seeming interested. It was raining steadily, a bone-chilling downpour. They raced to the Rabbit. Unlike Denise, Meg accelerated smoothly and swiftly through the gears. Nicky leaned back and relaxed.

They sat in bleachers that looked down on the

sale ring. The place was surprisingly crowded for such a miserable night. Rain pounded the steel roof. There was a stand for the auctioneer on the sawdust-covered floor where the livestock were paraded. Bawling calves, squealing pigs and bleating sheep were brought in — and sold off. As they gave voice to their confusion and fear of the unfamiliar place under the lights, of the auctioneer's loud spiel over the microphone, Nicky wanted to buy them all and take them to a safe place. Wild-eyed, they turned and twisted, searching for escape.

The ponies and horses were sold last. Brittle was not among them. Nicky blinked back tears. Not that the animals were being abused, but that they were chattel to be sold to the highest bidder — like TV sets — somehow seemed wrong to her. She knew the utter disregard for their sensibilities would be reflected in their physical treatment. Whether they were fed well or watered would depend on economic expediency.

Meg leaned toward her. "We can go now."

"I hate this place," she said, standing up and angrily jerking on her jacket.

"I do too. I can't let Brittle go through here. Can you?"

Nicky shook her head. If she had her way, she'd close the sale barn down.

XI

Nicky's parents had gone away to celebrate her mother's fifty-sixth birthday in August. But there was no escaping her father's birthday party, planned for October fourteenth. Her mother expected the children to attend — the invitation a command. Her father would be sixty-six.

"I can't believe he's closer to seventy than sixty," she said to Natalie as they bounced along in Nicky's truck.

"I always thought he was older than God." He

had been nearly forty-six when Natalie had been born.

"I suppose. You probably thought the same of me."

They turned the corner of Old Orchard Road and pulled into the driveway of the two-story brick house laced with ivy. There were five bedrooms and two baths upstairs, a huge kitchen, small library, large living room, dining room, and half-bath downstairs, wraparound porch out front, and a screened-in porch on the back. The house sat on a well-tended acre lot with decorative shrubbery and carefully spaced trees.

When Nicky walked in the side door, she was assaulted with memories. The warm and redolent kitchen brought past holidays to mind.

Her brother, wearing a half-smile, leaned against the door frame between the kitchen and the dining room. Broad-shouldered and tall, like his father, he wrapped himself in a protective cloak of cynicism. Mimicking the sound of a trumpet, he announced in a friendly voice, "The princesses have arrived to celebrate the royal birthday."

"Thanks for the welcome but if we're princesses, you're the prince. You've been living off the royal hospitality longer than I have," Natalie shot back, her affectionate tone softening the words.

His half-smile remained. "I moved out, cupcake, or hadn't you heard?"

Nattie punched him lightly on the shoulder and retorted, "Well, congratulations on your coming of age."

"It was lonesome without your caustic comments."

Her sister Nancy's two kids skidded into the

room, then turned and ran out in full shriek. From another room Nancy's raised voice reached Nicky's ears. "You want to run, go outside."

Jerry's reply, "Aw, let them have fun," reminded Nicky that she had never heard Nancy's husband support her in even the most reasonable requests.

"You heard your mother. You want to run or roughhouse, you go outside. You're in Grandma's house now."

"Grandma Cleo knows how to handle Jerry," Natalie said under her breath.

Neil added, "Yeah, she ignores him."

Nicky imagined the meaningful look her mother probably threw in Jerry's direction.

"Maybe we should just take them home, Nancy," Jerry suggested. He never challenged Nancy's parents. He talked around them.

"You go ahead. I'm staying," Nancy replied, and Nicky felt like cheering.

She lifted her thumb in silent approval and Natalie muttered, "He's such an asshole."

"For once we agree on something," Neil said.

Their father entered the kitchen, effectively ending further remarks about their brother-in-law. "Smells good, doesn't it?" he boomed, hugging his daughters. "Your mother never lets me forget this day. I think she just uses my birthday as an excuse to get you kids home."

Her mother had fixed ideas about holidays. She considered her husband's birthday a time when wife and children should gather round him with gifts and good wishes — perhaps to get him through the prospect of being another year older. Nicky couldn't fault her. The thought of turning forty alarmed her.

When they gathered for dinner, Jerry sat at the far end of the table with Nancy and the kids at his side. Her father presided over the proceedings from the other end.

"Grandpa, did they shoot the turkey?" Jordan asked, his dark hair hanging in his eyes.

"Don't talk about it," Jody said. She took aim at her brother with her fork.

"I don't really know, Jordan, but your sister's right. It's not a good topic for dinner-table conversation. Pick another." Her father sliced the turkey into edible portions and heaped it onto plates which were passed around the table.

"Maybe they ran over him with a car like that cat we saw coming here." Jordan stared at his plate, distaste curling his lip.

"Yuck," his sister said. "I'm not hungry. Mama, make him shut up."

Jerry took his son's plate away and said, "Just sit there and watch us eat then and try to be quiet for a change."

The boy burst into tears.

Her mother said in a calm, authoritative voice, "Give him back his plate, Jerry. I'm not going to have anything spoil this day. If he doesn't want to eat the turkey, he doesn't have to."

Watching this tableau, Nicky couldn't help thinking that the day was already well on its way toward ruin. A typical family get-together, she thought. "When is your mother going to bring you and Jody out to ride Tater?" she asked the boy, attempting to change the subject.

Jordan forgot his tears as his father put his plate,

minus the turkey leg, back in front of him. "Can we go, Mama?"

"Can we, Mama?" Jody echoed.

Nancy shot a grateful look toward Nicky. "Sure. Eat your food now."

"How's the horse business?" her father asked Nicky.

"Well, I suppose Mom told you we're down to Tater." She explained the situation.

Later, after the cake was eaten and the presents opened, Nicky and Natalie left. Darkness had fallen, a brisk, bright night shown by a harvest moon and a sky filled with stars. Nicky was thinking of Meg, who would soon leave for the Quarter Horse Congress in Columbus, Ohio. She had planned to show Brittle there, the largest breed horse show in the world, and instead was going in search of him. Denise was furious, and Nicky thought it was a futile move — because why would he be there if no Quarter Horse buyer would take him without papers?

Natalie broke into her thoughts. "I've been offered a job at Lakeview Country Club. It's a step up."

"You're not through with your classes yet, are you?"

"No, but I can quit the restaurant and work at the country club part-time. I don't think I want to get married."

Nicky shot her a quick look but Nattie's expression was hidden by shadows. "Did he ask?"

"No, but why do people get married anyway? To have children so that somebody'll be there for days like today? Look at the four of us. Would you want to have us for your kids?"

"What's the matter with us? We didn't turn out so badly."

"We just go home because we think we should. You and I are about as close as any of us get, and we were thrown together by them."

Feeling vaguely insulted, Nicky retorted, "It's nice to know that Mom and Dad are there. They should have had us closer together, is all. Then we might have found more in common."

"Maybe, and sure it's nice to know that Mom and Dad are always good for a loan."

"Natalie, I never ask for money from them." But she knew the financial safety net was under her. "And they support you."

"And through me, you."

Thoroughly annoyed, Nicky said, "Let's just drop it. Okay?"

In bed that night, she thought about how she struggled to keep herself independent of her parents. She was close to the end of her financial rope, though. The mowing was over, Brittle still gone, the horse photography on hold until the show season began again. When the unemployment checks stopped, Tater's rent and her parents' offerings for Natalie's room and board wouldn't be enough.

Panic gripped her, and she tossed sleeplessly. To put herself to sleep she often thought about making love with Beth. Their noon meetings on Wednesdays had become a weekly affair. But now she became embroiled in an argument with herself over their continuation. She had considered forcing Beth to make changes by refusing to see her unless she did. It had been Meg's idea.

* * * * *

"Don't invent any more stories just to see me," she said to Beth, who called her early Wednesday morning from the health club.

"I'll just tell the secretaries I'm going to meet you at your place for lunch. Mark'll be breathing my exhaust," Beth said. "Don't you want to see me?"

"I want to see you more than Wednesdays at noon and an occasional hour when Matt rides. I want to be able to call you when I need to talk. I'd like to go to a movie or a play once in a while or for a Sunday walk. It would be nice to have you over for dinner sometimes." Her heart thudded against her ribs, making her breathless.

Beth ended a long pause. "This is an ultimatum."

"Call it what you want. I've waited and waited."

"So you have, and I'm sorry. Maybe it's best not to see each other for a while. I'll call you, Nicky." The receiver clicked quietly in her ear.

"What's up?" Natalie asked, having just clambered down the stairs.

"Nothing." She stared at the phone as if it had betrayed her, hoping it might yet change its mind.

"You look sort of ghastly. You sure you're all right?"

Nicky nodded.

"Was it Beth?" Nattie shook Nicky's shoulder and looked into her face.

"I'm okay, Nattie." She made eye contact to reassure her sister. "I think I'll go for a walk."

"There's frost on the ground. Take a warm jacket."

She made footprints in the white covering, exposing grass limp and still green. By habit she had slung her camera over her shoulder, and she snapped Tater as he trotted toward her, his whiskers frosty. She took another picture of him shaking his lowered head at Scrappy, who briefly stood his ground barking. She filmed the swiftly flowing stream, cutting its dark, liquid path through whitened banks.

Her spirits lifted a little. She wasn't so beaten that she put her camera down. Now that Photoplay was supplying her with film and developing service in exchange for one day of work a week, she felt free to take as many pictures as she wanted.

She forgot all difficulties when she was using her camera, just as she did when she made love. Maybe she would never make love with Beth again. Her chest hurt as if something were stepping on it, flattening her heart, stomping the breath out of her lungs. She captured Scrappy and Tater drinking out of the creek. Scrappy had finally figured Tater's bluff. Tater took a step toward the dog and snorted, and Scrappy continued drinking even as a low, warning growl rumbled in his throat.

Nicky laughed and continued photographing them. It would make a great series, she thought. Then she straightened and looked out across the frosted grass toward the pale blue horizon. Winter was on its way — nights alone, holidays with the family, long, confining, cold days.

She went into the Fox Cities that morning and asked for a full-time job at Photoplay. It didn't matter if it wasn't what she wanted to do for the rest of her life. She didn't even care how much they paid for her services. "I know what I'm doing here, and what I don't know I'm well on my way to learning."

"We can pay seven an hour to start, but we may not be able to use you forty hours a week." The man in charge, Phil Jacobs, had dark stains on his fingers. His shirt was unbuttoned at the neck, the tie pulled loose.

"I don't care," she said. "Just put me to work."

She worked next to a heavy woman named Doreen Dombrowski who answered all her questions in knowledgeable detail, always supplying her with more information than she had asked.

"Want to go out after work for a drink?" Doreen asked at five o'clock. "I thought that thing was going to attach itself permanently to my ass," she said of the stool she spent each day sitting on.

"They're not exactly molded for comfort," Nicky agreed. She decided to take the time for a beer, not wanting to put off Doreen on her first day.

Doreen took her to a downtown bar. "Have you ever been here?"

Nicky hadn't. She looked around at all the trash hanging from the ceiling — ornaments from every conceivable holiday, along with plastic grapes and vines covered with dust. It gave her a closed in feeling. "Nope. What do you want? I'll buy."

A former high school science teacher, Doreen lived alone, divorced without children. She had a lively intelligence and shared stored-up trivia with anyone who would listen.

"What's your interest at Photoplay? Just a job?"

"I'm an amateur camera buff." Nicky asked her if she knew Margo, told her about her own work.

"I know Margo and that's why your name

sounded familiar. I can't believe this. You're Nicole Hennessey? Your work is wonderful."

Up till now Nicky had felt a little restrained and standoffish. Now she puffed up at the praise and found herself liking Doreen. She had to laugh at herself, taken in by flattery.

"But why are you at Photoplay? You should be free-lancing."

"I have to eat too, and pay the mortgage."

Meg returned from the Quarter Horse Congress on the last Saturday in October. Except for some oaks clinging to brown, rattling leaves, the deciduous trees were bare. Snow had already fallen once, a two-inch accumulation. She came to the farm before going home to Denise and let herself in after pounding on the door. "Anybody home?"

"Me," Nicky said, delighted to see her. Meg's cheeks were bright red, her gray eyes watery from the stinging wind.

Hugging her, Meg said, "You should have been there. I won't even try to tell you what it's like. The Congress is an experience, a microcosm. Got anything warm to drink?"

"Hot chocolate." Nicky put two cups of water to heat in the microwave.

That was when Meg told her she hadn't been home yet. "I want to ask you a favor. I'm going to leave Denise. When I do, I'll need a place to stay until I find my own. Would you put me up? I'll pay rent."

Nicky wrapped her arms around herself for

warmth. Wind shook the window panes. She was caught by surprise. "You're leaving Denise?"

Meg sat down at the table and put her hands around the cup of hot chocolate Nicky placed before her. "I've had lots of time to mull this over. I want out. I think I've wanted out for a long time. That's probably why I seduced you."

"Thanks," Nicky remarked dryly. "What was I? An experiment?"

"I'm crazy about you, Nicky. You're fun, you're kind, you're gifted. I could go on and on, but I don't want you to swell up and burst."

"And what's Denise going to say about your leaving? She'll blame me."

"Probably." Their eyes met in mutual assessment. "What will Beth say?"

"I did what you suggested and Beth said we should take a break from each other."

"Oh, Nicky, I'm sorry."

Feeling unexpected tears welling, she turned away. "It doesn't matter. I never had her anyway, just bits and pieces."

"Maybe that's the way to do it. It gives you some freedom. Sometimes being with someone is like having an albatross around your neck."

"How are you going to do this?" Nicky sat down and warmed her hands with the hot chocolate.

"I'll go home tomorrow. I'll sleep wherever you put me tonight. Denise doesn't know I'm back yet. This week I'll tell her I'm leaving. Next weekend I'll pack."

"That easy, huh?" Nicky smiled, just glad to be talking to her.

"No, I doubt if it'll be easy."

* * * * *

Off and on during the next three days Nicky thought about Meg, wondering if she'd muster the guts to leave Denise and what would happen if she did.

Tuesday after work Meg was waiting for Nicky in the kitchen. "It was too cold to wait outside. I didn't plan to come here, but I need some courage. I'm going to tell Denise tonight."

"Want something to eat?" Nicky always came home from work ravenous.

"I feel like I'm going to puke."

"Well, maybe you're not ready to tell her yet." Agreeing that Meg should leave Denise, Nicky decided to keep that opinion to herself. "You know you've got a bed here whenever you need it."

Meg left, white-faced and anxious, determined to make the break. Nicky understood. She herself was nervous about Denise's reaction, that she would be the target of her anger.

The next night she received an angry call from Denise. "Is this how you treat a friend, by taking her lover away?"

"Wait a minute," Nicky said. "I'm not taking anyone away. Let's get things straight here."

"She's not leaving me. You got that? No one's breaking up our relationship, especially not you." The receiver slammed in her ear.

When Friday arrived and Nicky had neither seen nor heard from Meg since Tuesday, she was uneasy for her. Doreen asked her out for a drink, and she went gladly. She liked talking photography with someone who knew something about it. She and

Doreen discussed shadows and angles, focusing and light, background and centering, and what made an interesting shot.

But when she drove in the driveway, the barn lot was cluttered with vehicles. Dan's truck was there, Meg's Rabbit, Denise's Toyota, and now her own truck. Natalie, she knew, was at work. Dan was standing between Denise and Meg. Nicky could hear their raised voices before she turned off the engine. She cringed at the confrontation.

"Now wait a minute," Dan was saying. "Just calm down."

"I'll fucking calm down when I feel like it," Denise shouted. "She's taken seven goddamn years of my life. I want them back."

"Oh, for Christ's sake," Meg said, throwing her hands up. "Don't do this here. Please."

Nicky stood on the fringes. She saw Meg's exasperation, Denise's rage, Dan's attempts to mollify them.

Denise gestured at Nicky, while shouting at Meg. "You been fucking her? Is that it? Is that why you want to move out? Be honest."

"Shut up, Denise. Just shut your disgusting mouth." Meg turned a pleading look on Nicky and Dan, as if to beg their understanding.

"Oh, so now I'm disgusting, am I?" She struggled to get past Dan at Meg, but he held her back with one large hand.

"Why don't we just cool down here and go inside and talk," he suggested.

"I'm leaving, that's why. I'll put your things out with the garbage Monday." Denise started toward her car.

"I'm going to get my things now." Meg opened the door of the Rabbit and turned to Nicky and Dan. "I'll be back later. I just want to get my clothes and show stuff. I am so sorry."

"You want me to come with you?" Nicky asked.

"Why don't you let her calm down first," Dan said.

"Because she isn't going to calm down. I'll call the police if I have to. It's better if I go alone." Meg followed Denise out of the driveway.

But she didn't return that night. She called around midnight, shortly after Nicky had fallen asleep. "I thought I was going to get the machine," she whispered.

"I can barely hear you."

"I don't want to wake Denise. But I didn't want you to worry, Nicky. I can't leave her alone tonight. I'm afraid of what she might do to herself."

"So you're not going to leave her?"

"Not tonight anyway. I can't apologize enough about what happened at your place today. Please tell Dan I'm sorry he got dragged into it, will you? I've got to go."

"Wait," Nicky said as Meg hung up. She had wanted to tell her to at least call tomorrow to let her know if she was all right.

XII

Having trouble making ends meet with her paycheck from Photoplay and only Tater's board, Nicky talked with Doreen about photographing events — such as weddings — during off-hours.

She framed a series of photographs and took them to Margo along with news of the proposed venture. Margo looked slimmer, healthier, and Nicky commented on her appearance.

"I'm happy. Being divorced agrees with me," Margo said cheerfully. Smiling, she studied Nicky's latest work. "I've missed you, Nicky. Don't ever stop taking pictures. These are wonderful."

Nicky basked in praise from someone qualified to give it. Had Meg said the photographs were wonderful, she would have been pleased but the compliment would have lacked impact.

"Look, I can book appointments for you," Margo offered. "It's the least I can do."

Doreen and Nicky ran an ad in the *Gazette*. Promising photography without intrusiveness, they named their fledgling enterprise Photo Perfect. A week went by with no response to the ad. Then one evening Janet Larson called on behalf of the State Quarter Horse Association, asking Nicky to film the Quarter Horse banquet in December.

"I remember you from the shows. Did Meg Klein ever find Skippy's Peanut Brittle?"

"Nope. We're still hoping he'll show up."

"I heard someone saw a horse that looked like him at the youth camp near Plainfield."

Meg had received many such calls — all of which she had followed up only to be disappointed. In her heart Nicky held little hope for Brittle's return. "Thanks, we'll check it out. And thanks for asking us to do the banquet."

"Will Meg be there? She was so high in the state points she's sure to get an award."

But not as All-Around Amateur. Nicky knew she had lost that chance when Brittle disappeared. "I'll get her there," she promised, thinking she might have to plead a need for Meg's help.

She started to call Doreen, then realized she didn't want to talk to her. Sitting in the darkened living room with a hand on Scrappy's head, she thought perhaps it was best when she worried about her finances to the exclusion of everything else. She had talked to Meg but hadn't seen her since that argument in the yard. Nor had she seen or talked to Beth. There had been several messages on the answering machine, with promises to call again, but she never asked Nicky to phone her.

Calling Meg at work the next day, she passed on Janet Larson's tip about Brittle.

"Tomorrow's Saturday. Let's go," Meg suggested.

"What about Denise?"

"She hates Brittle. It's been a nightmare, Nicky. All we do is fight. She wants to know where I've been, who I talked to, what I did every minute that I'm gone."

"Then why haven't you left?"

"When I say I'm leaving, she goes into rages, or she cries, or threatens suicide. I don't know what to do." She sighed and quietly said, "Someone just came into the lab. Got to go."

Nicky had to get back to work, too. As she sat on the stool next to Doreen, she thought maybe she shouldn't be so angry with Beth and just accept things as they were. Wasn't that better than being caught in a web like Meg was? And she missed Beth no less with the passing weeks. She longed just to see her, was desperate to talk with her.

Scrappy let out a soft woof as Natalie came into the house the next morning and headed for the stairs. In the still-dark room, Nicky glanced at the bedside clock. It was only six-thirty. Natalie spent several nights a week at Dan's now, sometimes leaving for school or work from there, sometimes returning to Nicky's for a change of clothes. Her mother would not like this, she thought. Wet with desire, she attempted to return to a quickly fading erotic dream but couldn't recapture it.

She got up, made coffee and let the dog out into the cold November morning. Shivering, she leaned against the counter in her robe, waiting for the liquid to seep through the ground beans.

"Did I wake you?" Natalie asked, coming into the kitchen fresh from the shower. She poured herself a bowl of Raisin Bran and sat at the table.

"That's okay. I needed to get up anyway. Meg's coming over early." She ran a hand through her tangled hair, then wiped the sleep from the corners of her eyes.

"How is she?" Natalie asked. "I still can't believe that scene in the yard."

"She's sorry it happened. So am I." Nicky poured them each a cup of coffee. "Your hair's still wet. You'll catch cold."

"I always thought Denise looked like a time bomb. I don't know what Meg sees in her." Natalie eyed her. "She guessed right about you two, though." Finishing her cereal, she pushed her chair back and bolted down her coffee. "Got to go. Say hello to Meg for me. Maybe you two *ought* to be together." Grabbing a jacket, she let Scrappy in as she went out the door.

Surprised because Natalie had never before offered an unsolicited opinion on her personal life, Nicky watched her go without comment.

A brisk wind accompanied Meg inside. She leaned against the door to force it shut. "Is it nasty out there! Looks like snow, feels like it, smells like it."

"You're an expert on the weather now?" Nicky asked, pleased to see her, realizing that she had missed her these past two weeks.

"I'm a meteorologist of the senses." Bending to pat Scrappy, she sat at the kitchen table. "I'd kill for a cup of coffee."

"No words of violence, please." Nicky poured them both a cup and began cleaning up the breakfast dishes. "Want something to eat?"

"I won't refuse a couple pieces of toast."

"So, how did you get away?" Nicky put bread in the toaster.

"I told her last night I was going with you to look for Brittle today," Meg said, her eyes surrounded by dark shadows, her cheeks hollowed.

"You look like shit, Meg, like you never sleep."

"Thanks. I love compliments."

"You want me to lie and say you look wonderful? What's going on?"

"She talks to me all night, asks me questions, wakes me up if I happen to fall asleep."

"What kinds of questions?"

"She asks about you and me. Were we sexual, do I love you, do I love her. If I find Brittle, am I going to sell him. When are we going to start looking for a house. Did I see you that day. Why do I like you. What do we do when we're together. Stuff like that."

Nicky frowned. "Are you going to move?"

"You sound like her. I don't know. She begs me to stay." Meg looked despondent.

"What about you? What do you want?"

Shrugging helplessly, she said, "I want to leave. You know that."

"Then you should." Nicky sat down and tried to meet her eyes. They were the color of storm clouds.

"I don't have a good enough reason, I guess. She makes me feel like such a creep." She slouched in the chair, spreading her long legs out in front of her.

After reflection, Nicky said, "Well, who am I to tell you what to do? What do I know?" Her own love life lay in ruins.

"I'm not giving you any more advice, either. I should have kept my mouth shut about you and Beth. You'd still be seeing each other."

"We'd still be spinning our wheels, too."

"That's better than not having any to spin," Meg remarked.

An hour later, as they were silently watching the countryside roll past the Rabbit's windows, Nicky had a sudden thought. "If this is Brittle, how are you going to claim him?"

"I have his papers and some pictures that you took."

Nicky had seen his registration. It only showed his color and markings, his sex and age, not how many hands he was or any scars. She wondered how willing anyone would be to give him up on the strength of Meg's word.

The long driveway into the camp cut through

sand-grown Norway pines, tall and stately. A small lake began where the road ended, a blue jewel whipped into white froth and surrounded by tree-blanketed hills. Meg drove to the log building marked "Office," and she and Nicky got out and knocked on the locked door. A cold wind swept grains of snow and sand around them, and they hunched into their winter jackets.

When no one opened up, they wandered through the deserted camp looking for some sign of life. Needle-strewn paths led them to the horse barn, where Meg explained their errand to a balding man in a heavy jacket and jeans. He looked at her doubtfully. "We moved the horses out of here a week ago. We farm them out during the winter months. When did he disappear?"

Meg told him and showed him Brittle's registration and the pictures of him.

"We did buy one horse a few weeks ago, a nice sorrel with some white on his face and legs like this one." He gestured at the photographs.

Nicky began to feel some of the excitement showing on Meg's face. They rode with the man, who introduced himself as Bill, in his Ford Explorer to look at the sorrel horse. Brief glimpses of sun shot through glowering clouds. Dirt from plowed fields mixed with snow and blew across the blacktop. Trees bent to the force of wind.

Bumping down a dirt driveway toward an old farmhouse and barn, she thought Brittle must feel right at home if he was here. It looked like her place with run-down fences and paint-starved buildings. She knew you had to have time and money to make improvements. Perhaps these people were like her, with a shortage of both.

Meg jumped out of the front seat. Nicky followed more slowly, not eager to feel the biting wind again.

Bill hollered, "Anyone around?"

A tall, lean figure appeared in the low door of the barn. "Hey, Bill. Come on in out of that wind. Bitter, ain't it?"

The three of them walked to the barn. The building offered shelter from the wind but no real warmth. Bill introduced them. "George, these ladies are looking for a stolen horse. Sounds like it could be that sorrel we farmed out with you."

Nicky stamped her feet on the cracked concrete floor to warm them. Cows mooed from a double row of stanchions behind George, who looked at Meg and Nicky with narrowed, flint-colored eyes. The farmer was so weathered his skin looked like grainy leather.

"I hate to see him go. The grandkids are safe on him," George grumbled as he examined Brittle's registration and studied the photographs. "Let's go look."

The horse stood in a large, barred stall at the far end of the barn. Chewing sweet-smelling hay, he looked up at them and nickered. Meg grasped the bars and peered into the dark stall, then shoved open the sliding door and stepped inside.

Nicky stood in the open doorway and watched. Although the horse appeared rough with a belly and a heavy coat of winter hair, she recognized him as Brittle. She sniffed back tears as Meg, sobbing, wrapped her arms around the animal's long neck and pressed her face to him.

"Guess it's him, huh?" the farmer said gruffly. "Never could understand why women get so emotional about an animal. Couldn't farm that way. Can't be crying when it's time to sell the stock."

Nicky thought he was addressing Bill, who looked uncomfortable and turned away from the tearful reunion. She waited to hear what Bill had to say, whether he would demand money for Brittle. "Do you have a bill of sale from the people who sold you the horse?" she asked.

He stuffed his hands in his back pockets and nodded. "But there's no identification on it, if I remember right, and they didn't want a check." He snorted a laugh. "We were stupid enough to give them cash. We paid five hundred dollars for that horse."

Nicky bit her tongue to keep from telling him what kind of money had been offered for Brittle. The horse continued munching hay, ignoring the drama of his discovery.

Kicking through straw bedding to stand next to Nicky, Meg said, "I'll give you two hundred and fifty as a reward. I can't afford any more than that."

Bill sighed deeply as he conceded, "That's better than nothing. I'll have to talk to the board members, but that's only a formality. I'm the director."

"When you gonna pick him up?" George asked dolefully.

Meg glanced at Nicky. "Tomorrow?"

She nodded.

With Brittle back in the field to keep Tater

company, Nicky felt a certain contentment, as if some things were as they should be. Tater's welcome caused them to laugh. Dan and Natalie joined Meg and Nicky at the fence to watch the horse and pony squeal, kick, buck, then race across the pasture together.

Natalie said, "If horses have strokes, I'd worry about Tater."

The two animals seemed immune to the cold. They could have sheltered themselves from the wind in the barn, but instead they grazed side by side on dead grass. When Nattie left with Dan in his truck, Meg and Nicky went into the house.

"Will you tell Denise?" Nicky asked, putting the morning's leftover coffee in the microwave. The kitchen windows steamed in the contrasting heat and cold.

While Meg paced the room, Scrappy sat under the table and turned his head from one to the other as they talked. "I wish I knew who took him. It could happen again, and next time they'd for sure sell him for meat."

"Well, Bill did give us a description of the people who sold him the horse." One of them had been a woman. A chill climbed Nicky's spine. "I can't hide him from Denise." She stood with a hand on her hip.

Stopping in mid-stride, Meg said, "You're a sexy woman, you know."

Nicky didn't know, and she was so taken aback by Meg's sudden reversion to sexual behavior that she couldn't make the transition immediately.

"I want you, Nicky. Let's go to bed." Meg's voice

became soft, almost pleading. She took a step toward her.

Startled, she said, "No." But as soon as she said it, she realized she wanted Meg too. "How come you're acting this way all of a sudden?"

"Why not? You're not seeing Beth. I'm not being sexual with Denise." She grinned suddenly. "And I love you."

Nicky felt herself blush. She still loved Beth, she was sure of it, but she had a strong emotional attachment to Meg too. Turning toward the microwave, which had beeped minutes ago, she hid her fluster by removing the coffee and pouring it.

"Look at me," Meg said from right behind her.

Startled, Nicky turned and found herself face-to-face with Meg, who took her hands. Her heart leaped into a fast, erratic beat. "What if Denise shows up?"

"We'll lock the doors."

"We can't. Nattie might come back."

"I don't care. I'll take the risk." She backed through the rooms with Nicky in tow, heading toward the bedroom. Meg gave a throaty laugh. "You'd think we'd never made love before. But this time we're going to do it right. No hurrying, no inhibitions."

Breathing in ragged, shallow gulps, Nicky felt as if her will had been taken from her. She stood stripped naked before she pulled the sweater over Meg's head. Watching the waves of hair fall back in place, she dropped the garment and combed her fingers through the pale, silken strands, then grasped Meg's face between her hands and kissed her.

Passion flowed between them, flaring when they touched. Nicky nibbled Meg's lips and felt the gentle thrust of tongue. They were still standing, pressed together, and fell locked in an embrace onto the bed when Meg lost her balance.

"Whoa," Meg said with a husky laugh. "You just swept me off my feet."

Nicky rolled on top of her and began a slow undulating motion with her hips. As always, she was enthralled by the softness of breasts against breasts, the smoothness of skin sliding against skin. She became entranced when kissing — the feel of warm, pliant lips, the taste of searching tongues.

The world outside the double bed faded. Even the dog's barking did not alert her immediately. Beth's voice calling for her from the kitchen and the sound of footsteps leading toward the bedroom shot a painful jolt of adrenaline through her. She felt as if she had experienced an electric shock, and she leaped to her feet in an explosive rush of energy.

Meg muttered, "Déjà vu."

Nicky thought she must be referring to Natalie's earlier discovery of them in bed, but this was different, much worse. Nicky shoved an unprotesting Meg into the closet with her clothes, straightened the bed and threw herself upon it — just as Beth opened the door. Raising on an elbow, she attempted to look sleepy.

"So here you are," Beth remarked as Scrappy sniffed her legs and wagged his tail, perhaps ashamed of his barking. She lifted a slender eyebrow. "Waiting for me?"

Nicky shook her head. Her heart beat wildly, as if trying to escape her chest. She told herself to cool it.

Attempting a slow, sensuous smile, she felt her lips quiver uncontrollably. "Why didn't you call?" she croaked.

"I haven't seen you in weeks. It seems like months. And that's all you have to say to me?" She moved closer to the bed.

Scrappy lost interest in her and smelled the closet door. Helplessly, Nicky watched him and prayed for Meg to remain silent.

"I saw Meg's car out there." Beth sat on the edge of the bed and pulled back the bedspread which covered Nicky's nakedness. "Mm, mm, mm. Look at you, sweetie." She ran her hand over the length of Nicky's body, which felt like a strung bow. "You don't seem particularly glad to see me."

Nicky stammered, "I'm just surprised is all." She frantically searched for a good reason to leave the bedroom, but her brain — frozen with fear — refused to function.

"Move over," Beth said, standing up.

Nicky, who had always loved watching her undress, stared with horror as Beth removed her clothes and slid under the spread. She asked, "Did you see Brittle?"

Beth turned on her side and wrapped Nicky in an embrace. "Did you find him?" She brushed Nicky's face with kisses.

"Yesterday," Nicky said, succumbing to the caressing lips in spite of herself. She realized that she was going to have to go through with this, because Beth would never forgive her if she found Meg in the closet. Equally disturbing was the way her body responded to Beth when only minutes ago she had been just as excited by Meg.

"You smell different," Beth murmured in Nicky's ear. "Using a new cologne?"

Again the adrenaline raced through Nicky, making her wonder how much stimulation her heart could assimilate. To divert Beth from her new scent, which could no doubt be attributed to Meg, she slipped out of Beth's embrace and kissed her neck, her breasts, her belly — moving toward the mound of dark curls.

"I don't want to do it that way. I want to see your face. I want to kiss you," Beth said, then gasped as Nicky's tongue touched her gently.

The first coupling was a frantic heads-to-tails. The second went slower, accomplished by the experienced touch of gentle, teasing fingers. They murmured their pleasure into each other's mouths, intermingling the words with kisses. Nicky forgot everything but the moment at hand, until she and Beth lay exhausted on the damp bed.

"Let's shower," she said, remembering Meg's hidden presence. Getting to her feet, she pulled Beth upright.

When they emerged from the shower and went outside, Meg waved to them from the pasture. She put Brittle into a slow canter and rode to where Beth and Nicky hung on the fence.

"Glad to see you back on a horse, Meg," Beth remarked.

"Thanks," Meg said, her eyes bright. "And it's good to see you here, Beth."

"It feels good to be here." Beth smiled at Nicky.

Nicky met Meg's gaze with a sheepish grin. A hot flush worked its way upward from her toes, suffusing her skin. Meg threw back her head and laughed, and Nicky, feeling terribly disloyal, laughed with her.

XIII

The snow swirls of the previous day were gone. Brittle had arrived home on a cold, sunny day. And Meg, sitting him bareback with Tater pressed against his flank, explained, "I just had to get on him for a few minutes."

"Well, now that we've said hello we're going inside." Nicky, ashamed by her outburst of laughter, added, "If you want to join us, feel free. It's frigid out here."

"I should go home," Meg said without enthusiasm.

Nicky knew that going home was on the bottom

of her list of places to go and things to do, but she needed to talk with Beth. Still, her heart went out to Meg. "You're always welcome. You know that."

Inside, she put some water on to heat and pulled out a couple of chairs at the kitchen table. Scrappy settled on her feet. He felt ridiculously light and wonderfully warm. "Why did you come here today?"

Beth shrugged and gave her a wistful smile. "I just couldn't stay away any longer. I'm on the other side of thirty-five and I've been sneaking around as if I'm a teenager. I told Mark I was going to see you."

Nicky got up to set cups of hot chocolate on the table. "What does that mean?"

"It's a step, don't you think?" Beth took a deep breath. "I thought I had more courage than I do. If I leave Mark, I have to start over in some other firm. I made some discreet inquiries. There's Robson, Brown and Jensen. They're women and they're interested in me. They handle a lot of divorces, custody cases, some personal injury, some criminal cases."

Reaching across the table, Nicky took Beth's hands in hers. Beth's efforts to break from Mark surprised her. Her own reaction surprised her more. She found herself questioning what she had thought she wanted, which was a live-in relationship with Beth. Having been on her own since leaving the university, she had never had to answer to anyone, hadn't had to temper her friendships. But she was jumping the gun. Beth hadn't suggested moving in with her, just finding a different place of employment. She should be enormously pleased.

"And Matt?"

Beth's eyes swam with tears, her chin quivered

and her voice shook. "I don't know. Maybe he won't even want to live with me." Looking down at her hands, she drew another deep breath. "We'll just have to see. I can't stay there for that reason alone. It's not healthy for him." She snorted. "It's not healthy for any of us. All that angry tension when Matt's within hearing, the fierce little fights when he's out of the room. It's an explosive situation."

Nicky was reminded of Meg and Denise. "If you move out, will you come here?"

"Nicky, I can't live with you. Please understand. Not right away anyway. If I have a place of my own, I might get Matt at least part of the time."

Hiding her relief behind sympathy, she replied quickly, "Hey, it's okay. At least we'll get to spend more time together, and we'll be able to talk on the phone whenever we want." They could do neither of those things now, not without covert action. Such freedom would feel like luxury. "How long can you stay?"

"What's for supper?" Beth grinned.

"Besides me?" Nicky inquired with an answering grin. "Ragu spaghetti."

"Even that sounds good. God, I've missed you. It got me going, this enforced separation. I wanted to have something to offer you when I saw you again."

"You sure surprised me," Nicky remarked wryly.

Now that Beth had made up her mind to move, she astonished Nicky by speedily putting her plans into action. She took the offer from Robson, Brown and Jensen, gave notice at Forrester & Forrester. She said over the phone, "I doubt if there ever would have been three Forresters on the sign." She had never told Nicky she wanted to be made a partner.

"Well, maybe there'll be a Forrester at the end of Robson, Brown and Jensen someday. Or are you taking back your maiden name?"

"I don't think so. I'm known in the profession by my married name."

Beth would be moving at the end of the month. She had found a two-bedroom apartment. Until then, she and Mark were sleeping in separate rooms and staying out of each other's way. She didn't want the expense of the house, she said. Matthew would stay with her only on weekends, which, Nicky realized, would limit her time with Beth to mostly weeknights.

December arrived and Beth's hired movers loaded her belongings in a Ryder truck during a snowstorm and carried them to her new place. Nicky and Meg helped unload and arrange the furniture to suit Beth. They moved the couch three times, the double bed twice, the hutch four times, the television to every wall and corner in the living room.

Nicky said crossly, "How can you make so many major decisions and not know where to put the TV? For Christ's sake, Beth, make up your mind. I'm worn out."

"I'll give you a massage later," Beth whispered in her ear.

"What about Meg?"

"She'll have to settle for pizza," Beth said.

Nicky looked at Meg's flushed cheeks and smiling gray eyes and became confused. She was happiest when Meg was with them. She wasn't sure when that had happened and didn't want to consider what it meant. She didn't admire Meg the way she did Beth, but she loved Meg's sense of fun.

There's always a snag, she thought. Where Beth was decisive, Meg waffled. It drove Nicky crazy to watch Meg make up her mind to leave Denise after a particularly bad fight, only to change it when Denise was contrite.

That night, while the wind howled mournfully outside the windows, driving snow in blinding sheets, Beth cried uncontrollably in Nicky's arms. Meg had departed early in order to feed and check on the horses and to make sure Natalie was around to take care of Scrappy.

"You can always go back to him," Nicky murmured, meaning only to comfort. She gave up any hope for the promised massage, sure that Beth had forgotten.

"You don't understand. I can't go back. I don't even want to," Beth wailed, her words punctuated by sobs. "I left my son. This is his first night without me." She curled into an inconsolable ball.

"I'm sorry." Nicky wondered why she had thought this would be a beginning for them. There was all this grieving to get through. Rolling onto her back, she put her arms over her face. Maybe they should just try to sleep. But hearing the wind beat snow against the windows, she got up and went to look.

The raging storm made her feel wrapped in a white cocoon. She hoped Tater and Brittle had had enough sense to seek shelter. Perhaps Meg had shut them in the lot with open access to the barn. She could see nothing beyond the moving wall of snow outside the glass, its cold penetrating the pane.

"I don't want you to think I'm blaming you, Nicky."

She turned to see Beth raised on an elbow, looking at her out of red-rimmed eyes. She had given a lot of thought to this and didn't hold herself responsible. "Beth, you can go against your nature only so long. You could stay and try to make Mark and Matthew happy, but it won't work if you're not happy, if it's not what you want."

"But maybe I didn't try hard enough." When Nicky shook her head and smiled sadly, she said, "I know you're right. I just feel shitty and selfish."

Nicky returned to sit on the edge of the bed. "Maybe this is kinder than hanging on and giving Mark hope and a half-assed relationship. He can find himself a woman who wants him."

Beth pulled her flat on the bed and kissed her. "You should have become a shrink."

"Oh sure." She laughed derisively, thinking that *she* was the one who needed counseling. Here she was with Beth, missing Meg. Did she miss Beth when she was with Meg? She tried to recall.

Beth rolled onto her stomach, holding herself up on her forearms. Tears gone, she looked at Nicky with loving eyes. "You know, we don't have to rush anymore. We can make love slowly and as often as we want. Do you think it will become less exciting?"

Nicky touched her nose. "It's red. Why is it so disturbing when someone cries?"

"I won't cry anymore tonight."

"Come here. Let's see if it's less exciting." She

recalled the heart-stopping lovemaking first with Meg and then with Beth as Meg hid in the closet. She hoped she didn't want that kind of excitement.

Nicky and Doreen put their heads together to decide how much and what kind of film to purchase for the Quarter Horse banquet. Nicky talked to Janet Larson about what was expected. Most of her photography had been shot outside. This would be inside at night. She had to guess right about lighting.

Meg rode with Nicky in her truck, leaving around eleven the second Saturday morning of the month. They drove to Doreen's apartment and she followed them to Pheasant Hill Resort north of Milwaukee.

While unloading their equipment and carrying it into the banquet hall, Nicky looked at the grounds surrounding the complex of buildings. She saw no wild game, just a well-groomed landscape with a swimming pool and golf course.

Nicky would not have recognized Janet Larson had she not met them inside the large room and introduced herself. She looked out of character in her dressy clothes. Several familiar-looking people were decorating and getting ready for the awards ceremony.

"It's good you're here early," Janet said.

"I'd like to take before, during and after shots," Nicky explained.

"What a good idea," Janet said. "I knew you were the right person to do this." She turned to Meg. "Glad to see you, too. I felt so bad when your horse disappeared."

"Thanks again for the tip. I just wish I knew who took him."

Janet remarked dryly, "I think we'd all like to know. It's hard to lock a barn."

Nicky began photographing. They had spent a lot of money on film, perhaps too much, but this job would give them an idea of what to charge. As the hall filled up, Doreen picked up a camera and also filmed. Meg took Doreen's job of jotting down the names of those photographed.

They paused briefly to eat. Then the speeches and awards presentation began. Meg had to stop taking notes long enough to accept three awards: a huge traveling trophy for Amateur Rookie of the Year, smaller ones for a third place in Amateur Western Pleasure and a fourth in Amateur Horsemanship.

During the accompanying applause, Nicky's camera lens blurred. When it cleared, she caught Meg's expression and thought it an interesting mix of emotions. But she didn't have time to ask her about her feelings until they were in the truck going home late that night.

"The support felt good, but I couldn't help thinking how different it might have been if Brittle hadn't disappeared."

"Maybe next year you'll be All-Around Amateur." Nicky caught glimpses of Meg in the passing headlights — her forehead and cheekbones, the halo of pale hair.

Meg grunted. "I just want to stop worrying about Brittle disappearing again. Did you like filming the banquet?"

"Yeah, I did." She could see herself doing that sort of thing for a living.

It was four a.m. when they reached the farm. In the windless night under a sky filled with stars, they stood briefly by the pasture fence picking out of the dark the forms of Brittle and Tater. Their breath froze on the icy air.

Nicky hadn't realized how tired she was until they went inside. Meg helped her carry in the camera, the bags of film, the tripod and extra lighting. They dumped it all in a corner of the kitchen while Scrappy danced a welcome around her.

"I'm not going home tonight," Meg said.

"It's awfully late. Why drive anymore?"

"Exactly. But I may not go home at all, except to get my things when Denise is at work."

Nicky wasn't in the mood for a discussion. "Let's talk about it tomorrow. There's the other bedroom downstairs here. It's got a lot of junk in it, but there's a bed. Why don't you sleep there tonight?"

The phone's insistent ringing dragged Nicky out of sleep, and Denise's voice demanding, "Let me speak to Meg," brought her instantly awake. Nicky looked at the clock. Six-thirty. Still dark.

"I'll get her." Crossing the living room to the other bedroom, she shook Meg awake.

"Tell her I'm not here."

"She knows you are. Come on, Meg, I don't want to be in the middle of this. Take it in the other room." Nicky hung up the bedroom phone and burrowed under the covers. The cold floors made her feet ache. Drafts chasing through the old house chilled the rest of her. She heard Meg's voice rising and falling, angry and plaintive.

Then Meg was sitting on her bed, waking her again. "She's going to tell the people at work."

"Tell them what?" Nicky asked, feeling drugged.

"That I'm a lesbian."

"What? You could do the same to her."

"She says she doesn't care, that she'll destroy me if I leave her." Meg looked desperate. "She makes scenes."

Nicky knew that. "So you stay with her?" she asked, incredulous.

"I don't know. Go back to sleep."

"I'm wide awake," Nicky complained. "Promise me something. That you won't leave here until I do get up."

"It's a deal."

A few hours later, after an exhausted sleep, one look told her that Meg had not closed her eyes since Denise's phone call. She had made coffee, though, and poured a cup for Nicky.

"Have you come to any decisions?"

"I'll stay here if that's still okay."

"It'll be nice to have you."

Beth, however, wasn't thrilled with the plan.

"She just needs a place to stay. And you won't

live with me," Nicky said defensively. They were at Beth's apartment.

"That's the problem. I'm not there."

"Oh, so no one should be with me. Isn't that generous of you?"

"Natalie's with you." Beth gave her an appraising look, which Nicky met. She capitulated. "Forget it. You're right. You shouldn't have to live alone."

Nicky reached for her. Her feelings were so torn between Beth and Meg that she was riddled with guilt. And right now, perversely, she wanted to be at the farmhouse just to make sure Meg had not acceded to Denise's demands that she go back to her.

"Let's go to bed, sweetie." In all the years that Beth had lived with Mark, she and Nicky had not actually slept together, had only climbed into bed to make love, had longed to fall asleep after the loving.

When the phone call came from Meg, Nicky half-expected to hear that she was returning to Denise.

"I'm sorry to bother you two, but something's wrong with Brittle, and Tater's deathly sick. I need help."

"Did you call the vet?"

"Yes. Just get here quick. Okay?"

"I'll come with you," Beth said as Nicky put on the clothes she had just removed.

"You have to work tomorrow."

"So does Meg and so do you. Or don't you want me to help?"

"Of course, I do. Meg said to hurry."

When Nicky and Beth burst into the barn, they

found Dan and Natalie, Meg and the veterinarian, Brittle and Tater, all standing among the empty stanchions. Tater's legs were trembling, and Brittle's head hung nearly to the cement floor. It looked like Meg had plenty of help. "What's wrong?"

The vet, who was rolling up a long stomach tube and putting it in a pail, answered her. "They're colicking. I oiled them." He turned to Meg. "I'll leave you some intramuscular pain medication. Keep them from rolling if you can. Call me if they get any worse. Time will tell now." An icy wind swept inside as he went out the door.

"We have to walk them," Meg said bleakly, "to keep them from going down. Tater's especially bad. We're going to need a lot of help if anyone's going to sleep tonight."

Dan seemed to be holding the pony on his feet by sheer force. "I don't know if he's going to make it."

Puzzled, Nicky asked, "But why? What happened?"

Meg glared at her. "I wish I knew."

"Usually this occurs when they eat too much grain or alfalfa, or something moldy," Dan explained patiently. "Horses have small stomachs and miles of intestines. They get impacted easily."

Nicky thought she had never been so cold in her entire life nor endured such a long night. Even with five of them rotating, two hours at a time, she was exhausted from the frigid temperatures and the physical effort. And Meg refused to leave Brittle for more than a short break. They dragged the horse and pony up and down and around the stanchions, whipping them to their feet whenever they went down and tried to roll.

"Why can't they rest?" Nicky asked, crying from fatigue and the pain she had to inflict. Tater's legs had just crumpled under him.

"They can as long as they don't thrash around. They twist their intestines that way, and once that happens, they're goners. Who knows? Maybe they already have." Meg tugged on Brittle's lead rope.

Toward morning, on her second shift with Meg, Nicky asked, "How much longer do we have to do this?"

"Until they start passing whatever they ate."

"Is that going to happen?" Tater staggered at the end of the lead. He stumbled and once more sank with a groan to the cold floor.

At first light the veterinarian, a small, neat man, entered the barn with Dan behind him. He examined Tater first, looking at his eyes and gums. "He's in shock." He listened to the pony's distended gut. "Nothing moving." He looked at them. "Has he passed any manure?" They shook their heads in unison and he nodded grimly. "It's time to make a decision about whether he should suffer anymore."

"We used up all the medication," Meg said dully, continuing her endless trek around the barn. Brittle paused and passed a pile of manure and they stared at it as if it were manna from heaven.

While Nicky and Beth watched, the veterinarian injected a solution into Tater's bloodstream, ending his pain and his life. Pressed against the wall, Meg stood with Brittle on the far side of the barn. Dan helped the vet. Natalie chose to stay inside the house.

It was not horrible to watch. The pony apparently died peacefully and quickly, but Nicky couldn't stop crying. Beth put a comforting arm around her. She cried harder.

Exhausted but out of danger, Brittle fared better. The veterinarian said it was a wonder he hadn't foundered, said the pony would have been crippled by founder. Dan phoned the person who removed dead stock, then left when the vet did.

Shortly afterwards, Beth drove to her apartment to get ready for work, and Nicky and Meg went into the house together. The warmth released the cold in her, causing her to shiver and her teeth to chatter.

"I'm calling in sick," Meg announced. "I need to keep an eye on Brittle."

"You can't watch him every minute," Natalie said from the doorway, looking as if she had been crying too.

"Did you see anyone out here yesterday?" Meg asked her.

"Only Denise. She was looking for you, Meg."

Meg looked baffled. "Denise doesn't know anything about horses. She's scared of them."

Suddenly realizing what a dolt she was, since it hadn't occurred to her until now that foul play might have been involved, Nicky asked, "Do they do autopsies on horses? Maybe we need to know what they ate."

Looking at Nicky with respect, Meg said, "I should have thought of that myself."

"I'll call Dan so he can cancel the meat wagon," Natalie said, heading toward the phone. "Nicky, you better get Beth's permission."

XIV

The autopsy report told the story. The animals had been fed a sweet feed, which had expanded in their guts — in the pony's case, proving fatal.

Now it was Brittle who was lonesome, who ran to the pasture fence whenever anyone was outside, who nickered for company. Listening to him, Nicky ached for the loss of Tater, for knowing that someone had willfully caused his death. Had Brittle been the target? Tater merely the victim? She couldn't forget how he had collapsed from the pain, his only complaint an occasional grunt.

Meg, tired and thin, continued a grim watch on Brittle. She hadn't gone back to Denise, had been forced to leave many of her belongings in the apartment because Denise had changed the locks. Fortunately, she had gotten most of her clothes out.

Nicky wondered how long Meg would be able to maintain the pace she was keeping. She set her clock so that she would awaken every two hours during the night, left at the last possible minute to get to work on time and came home immediately afterwards. The fun-loving part of her had vanished as it had during Brittle's disappearance. No longer did she try to seduce Nicky, nor did she seem even vaguely interested in anything but safeguarding her horse.

The holidays passed in a blur of family get-togethers. January took forever, and now February was halfway over. Nicky always started looking for spring when March arrived, figuring warm weather was finally in sight.

But this particular day looked like winter would never end — gray, windy, dismally cold, no sign of green anywhere. She stood by the kitchen window, sipping coffee and watching Meg work out by the barn.

"What are you thinking, sweetie?" Beth asked from the table. They alternated weeknights between the apartment and the farm.

"I'm tired of the cold."

"Maybe next year we can take some vacation time and go south for a week or two."

Nicky turned and forced a smile. "That would be nice."

"You have a wedding to photograph this weekend?"

She nodded. "What are you going to do?"

"Watch Matt swim or something."

"He's the most organized kid I ever knew. What happened to free play?"

"He likes organized sports," Beth said. "Is Meg going to help you?"

"You ought to know better. Meg never leaves Brittle, if she can help it."

Beth wrapped her hands around her coffee cup and gazed at Nicky. "You're not happy with our arrangement, are you?"

Heart thudding, Nicky only shook her head and looked away. She felt restless and entangled, but she couldn't tell Beth. She was cowardly, she knew. Toward the end of the week she always looked forward to the weekend when she could spend time alone with Meg. But by the time Mondays rolled around, she was again missing Beth. She didn't understand her ambivalence toward the two of them.

Beth broke into her thoughts, "Someday we'll live together."

Nicky shrugged, helpless to explain her feelings. She could see Meg dumping feed into Brittle's tub, opening the gate to the pasture. Denise had been over yesterday evening, as she had every night for at least the past month, and before that she had called every day since Tater's death. Denise was either cajoling or attacking. It all exhausted Nicky, and she wondered why Meg put up with her angry appearances.

"You're just a fountain of conversation this morning, sweetie. Something on your mind?"

Meg was now coming toward the house, her head down, shoulders forward. Depressed, Nicky thought.

"Nope." She moved away from the window as the door opened. Frigid air rushed into the room.

When Beth was ready to leave for work, Meg looked up from her place at the table. "How do you like working with all those women?"

"I love it." Beth moved toward the door, briefcase in hand, casually elegant with her London Fog over a pinstriped, worsted wool suit.

Like my mother, Nicky thought. Was that what had attracted her to Beth? Cold air once more swept into the kitchen with Beth's departure.

"You must be on top of the world, Nicky. Everything's working out for you." Meg sounded as glum as she looked. She stared into the blackness of her coffee.

"You're running out of steam. You know that, don't you? Burning the candle at both ends."

Meg's gray eyes cleared. "And you're full of cliches."

Nicky shrugged. "Well, they fit. Look, life should center around more than a horse's welfare and a harassing ex-lover." She gave Meg an appraising look and asked the question that had been bothering her for months: "Where was Denise the night Tater died? Did you ever ask her?"

"I've got to get ready for work." Meg glared at Nicky before leaving the room. "I told you, Denise doesn't know anything about horses."

Nicky jumped up and followed her. "I hate what's happening to you." Then she quietly admitted, "I miss the old you."

Meg talked over her shoulder. "Whoever gave the horses that moldy sweet feed probably kidnapped Brittle. Denise was with us when that happened."

Nicky persisted, "Someone's been turning off the camera out by the barn. You and Beth and Natalie and Dan are the only ones who know it's there." She had set up a hidden video camera the day after Tater's death.

Shrugging, Meg turned away. "It probably turns itself off when the tape is full."

"I change it every six hours. Why do you turn it off, Meg?"

"Don't you get tired of looking at that tape?"

Actually, she hadn't been looking at it. She had watched it for a few weeks after first installing the camera. Then, after falling asleep while viewing the videocassette, she decided to scan it only if something suspicious happened. Otherwise, she would just tape over the previous six hours. "Do you want me to take it down?"

Meg stood against the bathroom door frame, chewing on her lower lip and frowning. "It's your camera. It's your barn. Do what you want."

"You still haven't told me why." Standing close to Meg, she became aware of her odor — the freshness of her skin and hair, the faint smell of cologne, even the trace of horse wafting from her clothes.

"You wouldn't understand," Meg said flatly. "I've got to shower now."

Nicky grabbed her arm. "Try me."

Meg looked at the restraining hand before lifting her gaze to meet Nicky's. Her eyes narrowed and clouded. "I don't want to know. Would you want to think that of Beth?"

"Beth wouldn't do that." She released Meg's arm.

Clattering down the stairs, Natalie headed past them toward the kitchen. "What's going on?"

Nicky trailed after her sister. "I didn't even know you were here last night. I haven't seen you for days."

"I came in early this morning to study, then fell asleep again." She poured herself a cup of coffee and popped two pieces of bread into the toaster. She gave Nicky a speculative look. "You two having a disagreement?"

Feeling tired, Nicky rubbed the back of her neck. "Meg's been turning off the camera out by the barn."

"I could have told you that," Natalie said with raised eyebrows.

"Why didn't you?" Nicky snapped.

"It wasn't any of my business." She spread peanut butter on the toasted bread and took a bite. "I've been thinking about it, though. She doesn't want to believe Denise did it, does she?"

"Do you think she did?"

Natalie finished eating the toast and licked her fingers. "I don't know. What do you think?"

Nicky realized that she wanted Denise to be guilty, if only to finally free Meg of her. "I don't know either."

March blew itself out in a gale. Eight inches of snow fell, covering bits of promising green. Nicky had gone to Margo's after work to collect a check and show her her latest work. Now she crept along the country roads toward her farm, hoping she wouldn't end up in a ditch. It reminded her of the storm the day Beth moved into her apartment.

She thought of Beth, her recurring bouts with sadness and guilt. During the first weeks after Beth left Mark, Nicky had thought she might capitulate and go back to him. She told Nicky the only thing that kept her from doing that was knowing that if she did she could never leave again, at least not until Matt grew up. Tonight Beth was having dinner with one of her firm's partners, Nancy Brown, with whom she was working on a case.

She wanted to ask Meg when she was going to start showing Brittle again. That had bothered her since Janet Larson had called to ask her if she was going to be at a March show. She had been surprised to learn that the show season had started. Janet had told her that there were shows as early as January at indoor arenas.

The road had deteriorated to two narrow lanes. Drifts rose on either side of her where open fields stretched away in both directions. The wind, barreling out of the northwest, rocked the truck. She wondered if she would be able to get into her driveway, if she'd be lucky enough to get that far.

But an hour after leaving the Fox Cities, a drive which normally took twenty minutes, she drove slowly toward the barn between ridges of freshly plowed snow and silently thanked Dan for taking the time and making the effort to dig her out.

The wind hit her with tremendous force as she struggled toward the house, pausing only briefly by Brittle's lot to make sure the gate was closed. She assumed he was shut in his stall, and the wind pushed her in the direction of the back door.

Winter in Wisconsin was an adventure, she thought as she pulled the storm door closed behind her. Scrappy waited just inside, and she patted him as he danced his welcome. The warmth of the house enclosed her, giving her back the breath that the cold and wind had snatched from her. She loved the snow, the excitement of a storm, the coziness of being inside while the elements raged outside.

She had parked next to the Rabbit, buried under several inches of snow, recognizing it by its shape. Only the stove light was on and she pressed the flashing red button on the answering machine. Natalie told her that she was at Dan's, that if she needed either of them to give a call. Doreen said they had a fiftieth wedding anniversary party to film a week from Friday evening. Margo called to tell her one of the prints she had just brought in had already been sold to a neighbor. Lastly, her mother spoke from Florida, where she and Nicky's father had gone to escape storms such as this one. After rewinding the tape, she went in search of Meg.

"Nicky, come on in. Don't go sneaking out on me."

She had been closing Meg's bedroom door quietly behind her, thinking her asleep. "I'm sorry. I didn't mean to wake you up." She stood uncertainly in the doorway.

Meg patted the blanket, urging her to sit. "What a storm, huh? Dan was plowing the driveway when I got here. He put Brittle in the barn. You have trouble getting home?"

"Some." Nicky lowered herself gingerly onto the bed and Meg shifted her weight to accommodate her. "Looks like we're snowed in."

Meg smiled with some of her old mischievousness. "Alone, together."

"You didn't hear any of those calls on the machine?"

"I listened. I just didn't feel like talking to anyone. Where's Beth tonight? With Matt?"

"With a colleague."

The phone interrupted their conversation and they listened to the four rings, to Nicky's taped message, to Denise's voice. Nicky sat in frozen silence, watching Meg's expression.

Meg rose on her elbows, the blankets falling to her waist. She was fully dressed in a white, work uniform.

"If you're there, Meg, answer the phone. I know you're not at work, because I called. I just want to know if you're safe. Give me a ring."

She sounded like a perfectly normal person making a reasonable request. Nicky sometimes wondered whether Denise was a little crazy. When Meg fell back on the bed and turned her head toward the wall, Nicky got up. But as she turned away, she felt a hand close over her wrist.

"She spoils everything."

"She has a talent for that." Nicky looked down at her, at the fair hair fanned out on the pillow. Even as she told herself not to do it, she found herself back on the bed, taking Meg in her arms.

Nicky didn't pause to wonder about the passion that flared between them. They struggled to remove their clothes without getting out of bed, throwing the discarded items in a heap on the floor. Moving on top of Meg, she began the circular pelvic thrust that excited her so. Their kisses, at first just a soft touch of lips, grew hot and deep and wet.

Then Meg rolled her until they lay side by side, face to face. Running a hand over Nicky's bare length, she slid cool fingers into the tangle of hair and raised a knee to push them inside.

Nicky, who had been about to reach for Meg, paused to enjoy the sensation. She sucked in air as Meg slowly withdrew the fingers and began a gentle stroking. An exquisite ache tugged in her groin, stirring her into motion again. She looked into Meg's gray eyes, now hooded with desire, her mouth twisted in a sensual smile. Smiling in response, she closed her eyes and arched her back.

To stave off climax, she covered the space between Meg's legs with her hand and gently worked her fingertips through the damp hair. "You are so wet," she murmured, sighing as she fingered the sensitive leaves and folds of flesh.

Their free arms held them close to each other, and Meg's throaty laugh filled her ear. "So are you."

"God, who wouldn't be." The words came out sounding like a moan.

Raising herself on an elbow, Meg bent to take Nicky's nipple in her mouth and Nicky fell back once more. She felt the tugging at her breast in her groin, and when Meg thrust inside her, she raised her hips in response.

But she couldn't resist asking, "Why aren't you showing?"

"What?"

"Janet told me the shows started months ago. You haven't gone to any." Why was she pointing this out now, she wondered as the pleasurable ache lost its throb.

Sighing, Meg lifted her head from Nicky's breast and looked at her. "Can't we talk about this later?"

But Nicky had experienced a sudden flash of insight. That was why she had to say, "You don't want to do too well, do you?"

"It's been too damn cold to show. Brittle's still got a winter coat. Those people who show in the winter keep their horses blanketed and under lights." Meg rolled onto her back.

"But I should be at those shows. Why didn't you say anything?" Nicky asked.

"I didn't think of it."

"You have to go with me anyway, even if you don't take Brittle."

Meg turned to face her, tucking her knees up in a fetal position. Idly she stroked Nicky. "Want to finish this?"

Nicky met her gaze with a crooked smile. "I'd be a liar if I said no."

"Say please, then."

"How was your weekend? Your dinner Friday night?" Nicky greeted Beth as they walked toward the farmhouse on Monday afternoon. It was unusual for them to arrive home together.

"All right. We're having another dinner meeting tomorrow night. Maybe you'd rather stay here than wait at my apartment for me."

Nicky was looking around, marveling that the snow was gone except for a few solitary, shaded clumps. She opened the back door for Beth and fended Scrappy off with attention. "Can't you get your work done during the day?"

Beth's heels clicked across the kitchen floor, and Nicky admired the swing of her hips. "There are going to be a lot of after-hours. It goes with the job."

In the bedroom she watched Beth remove her clothing as she changed her own, putting on jeans and a flannel shirt. They might have been making the bed, she thought, they were so used to each other. Was that good? Meg's long, athletic body walked into her thoughts.

"Sweetie, we have to talk."

"Hmm? What about?" She sat on the bed as Beth hung up her clothes.

"There's a conference week after next in New York. I'm booked to go."

Nicky frowned a little. "All of a sudden there are a lot of meetings."

"I know. Nancy Brown wants me to participate fully in the firm."

"Don't the other partners?"

"Yes, of course they do. It's just that I'll be going to the conference with Nancy."

"She's a lesbian, isn't she?" She spoke in a flat voice, her heart hammering at her own guilty behavior, expecting the same from Beth.

Beth nodded and turned away to hang up her suit. "But that's beside the point. I hope you'll understand."

Her jaw clenched. "It's just going to be the two of you at these dinner meetings and the conference?"

"I love you, Nicky. This is business," Beth replied, her back still turned.

Well, what could she say? What had she done over the weekend but muddy the waters with Meg? Somehow, though, she didn't want Beth doing the same. Envisioning Beth opening herself to another woman nauseated her. She followed her to the kitchen. In Natalie's absence, Beth did the cooking.

"Tell me about your weekend?"

Startled, Nicky looked for telltale signs of Beth's knowledge of her infidelity. "I went to a horse show on Sunday."

Removing a package from the refrigerator, Beth began deboning chicken, performing the task with a proficiency Nicky admired. "Did Meg show Brittle?"

Stir-fry, Nicky remembered, and started chopping vegetables. "No, but I took my camera and sold some photos." Slicing her finger instead of the green pepper, she wrapped a paper towel around the injured digit and continued, "Meg has missed a bunch of shows. I think she's maybe afraid Brittle will get snatched again if he wins too much."

"If you buy that theory — that he was kidnapped because Meg was too successful with him."

"True." Peeling away the bloody toweling, she sucked her finger.

"Only you, Nicky, would mistake your finger for a vegetable." Beth had finished deboning and turned her attention to Nicky. "Let's get a bandage on that."

"I can do it."

"Let me. You'll bleed all over everything. You shouldn't be allowed in the kitchen except to eat and clean up." Beth grasped the injured member. "This is a lovemaking finger. Don't be so careless with it."

Nicky laughed. "I guess I'll have to use other parts of my anatomy."

In bed that night after making left-handed love, her tongue tired and her lips slightly swollen, Nicky lay awake staring at the shadowy ceiling. Doubts were sinking in slowly, twisting her guts, flooding her with panic and nausea. Beth, who lay in lovely slumber next to her, her long lashes gracing pale cheeks, looked the part of wronged lover. But Nicky couldn't shake the niggling worries that she, herself, was being cheated on.

Tossing and turning for hours before falling into a restless sleep, she woke up tired and vaguely angry with the woman lying next to her, as if she were the one responsible for her fatigue.

XV

Nicky stood with one foot in the fence, watching Meg ride. There was an exciting warmth in the wind that played across her face, bringing an earthy smell on its current of air. But she couldn't appreciate the signs of spring around her or settle anywhere for very long or concentrate for more than a few minutes. Beth was in New York, and Nicky was certain she was sleeping with Nancy Brown.

She had seen it in her eyes after every dinner meeting, a glazed expression that she thought had been reserved for herself, a sort of afterglow. Her mouth twisted as she recalled their conversation over the phone last night, when she had said accusingly, "I called your room around midnight last night. You weren't there."

"I was out."

She had turned sarcastic. "Were you still out at three o'clock this morning? Because I called then too."

There had been a long silence before Beth said, "I turned the sound down on the phone. I guess I didn't hear it ring. Why would you call me in the middle of the night anyway?"

Why would Beth admit to any wrongdoing? And why would she, Nicky, want to hear about it if she did? Considering her own behavior, what right did she have to question Beth? But it was like poking at a sore tooth with her tongue, unable to leave it alone no matter how painful.

Meg rode toward the barn, cooling Brittle off at a walk. Her body moved with the rhythm of the horse. As they reached the gate, she smiled and winked at Nicky. "When you going to learn to ride, woman?"

An unexpected flush rose up Nicky's neck. Meg never failed to turn her on with her athletic grace, her flirtatious behavior. "Never. I like a ground's-eye view."

"Let me practice opening the gate," Meg said as Nicky started to do it for her. Opening a gate on horseback was part of the trail class.

The warmth of the April day faded with the setting sun. Meg and Nicky fixed dinner together. Neither being adept in the kitchen, they decided to thaw and bake a pizza and prepare a tossed salad.

Scrappy, parked at his favorite spot under the

table, was the first to hear someone at the door. With a bark he rushed to investigate and confronted Denise, who knocked and let herself in at the same time and then turned rigid at the sight of the dog.

Sighing, Nicky said, "He won't hurt you, although he might lick you to death. Scrappy, go lie down." And to Denise again, "Come on in. We're just fixing something to eat. Care to join us?" Nervy, she thought, walking in like this. She deserved to be bitten. Why on earth had she invited her to stay?

Denise eyed the little dog until he settled under the table. "Thanks, but I'm not hungry," she demurred, her tone uncharacteristically soft, her eyes fixed on Meg.

Nicky looked from one to the other, sensing Meg's dismay.

"Can I talk to you alone?" Denise addressed Meg.

Meg clutched the pizza she had been about to pop in the oven, her rapidly beating pulse visible in her throat. "Where?"

"How about your room? You do have your own room, don't you?" A little sharpness crept into her tone.

"Sure," Meg agreed. "Just let me put this in to bake."

Nicky listened to the sound of their voices, rising and falling, as she absently ripped apart a whole head of lettuce. "How are we going to eat all of this?" she said aloud and felt Scrappy's nose against her leg. She looked down at him. "You don't like it when people fight, do you?"

It was pitch black outside the kitchen window and suddenly silent inside. She strained for sounds from the bedroom and heard nothing at first. Leaning on the counter, she listened harder and thought she detected sobbing. What the hell, she thought with exasperation. Who was crying and why?

She heard the door being flung open and Meg's voice, choked and angry. "Get the hell out of here."

Unable to move, she turned to watch Denise shuffle through the kitchen, the back door closing quietly behind her. She had never thought she would feel a pang of pity for her, but now she did. She shot a questioning glance at Meg.

Meg looked furious. "So go ahead and say you told me so."

"Why don't you just tell me what's going on?"

"She did it. She gave them the sweet feed. She swears she just fed it to them to get them out of the way. She said it was in an open bag in the feed room in a corner, and she wanted to divert them while she walked to the stream. So she dumped it in the tub and shut them in the lot."

Nicky frowned. "There *was* an old bag of Dan's feed in there," she said in a quiet voice, seeing it in her mind's eye. It had been just where Denise said it was. "She could be telling the truth." But why would she walk to the creek on such a bitterly cold day?

"She should have told me this a long time ago."

"If you'd been her, would you have admitted it? After Tater died?" Nicky unwillingly played the devil's advocate.

Scrappy startled them by again rushing to the door in full bark. "If that's Denise, tell her to get lost," Meg said as Nicky went to check the door.

"There's a trailer up the road by Dan's," Denise announced breathlessly. She looked wild in the meager light flowing out through the open door.

"Would he be taking a bunch of his cows somewhere this time of night?"

"I thought he only sold off the bull calves." Meg turned to Nicky.

"Dan's not even home. He and Natalie went to a movie tonight," Nicky said. "Are you sure, Denise?"

She stood just inside the door, her hair disheveled and her pupils enormous. "It's a great big trailer behind a semi, and some people are loading cattle in it. I could see them. I could hear them."

Nicky met Meg's eyes. It was all she needed to believe Denise. "Rustlers?" It happened. She'd read about it in the paper. "Let's go."

"Denise, you call the sheriff. Okay?" Meg grabbed a jacket from the back hall. She patted Denise on the shoulder. "Good work, woman."

"Don't let Scrappy out," Nicky said, holding the dog inside with one hand.

"Hey, they might have guns," Denise protested. "Wait while I call, will you? I want to go with you."

"What now?" Meg asked, following Nicky to her truck. "Maybe we shouldn't do anything."

"I can't not do anything. Dan's done too much for me. Let's just drive out there. Maybe they'll go away." They stood under the dusk-to-dawn light. Excitement made her heart hammer, her legs feel weak.

"If they go away, they'll take what they've got in the trailer."

"Not if we park my truck in front of theirs."

"Nicky," Denise called from the house, her thin figure silhouetted in the light behind her. "Can you tell them how to get out here?"

"Jesus," Nicky muttered, doubly disgusted as the

dog brushed past Denise and made a dash toward them. She grabbed the phone and gave directions. "The tractor-trailer rig is parked in front of Paulson's Dairy Farm. How soon can someone be here?" she asked the dispatcher at the sheriff's office.

"Fifteen minutes outside. Don't go playing heroine and queer it for us. We think we know who these guys are."

Strange choice of words, she thought, hanging up the phone and turning slowly toward the other two women who had joined her in the darkened dining room. "He told us to stay out of it, but we can't just let them escape."

They compromised by driving the truck, lights off, to the end of the drive where they could keep the tail end of the trailer in view. The cool night closed around them. The plaintive mooing of the cattle reached their ears. A screech owl called eerily from somewhere close by. Scrappy barked from the house behind them.

Peering down the road, the women watched the rustlers' progress with strained eyes. Five minutes passed without any of them exchanging a word, which was a goddamn miracle, Nicky thought. After five more minutes the last of the animals were loaded and one of the shadowy figures started to close the tailgate on the livestock.

"Anyone wants out better vamoose now," Nicky said quietly, her pulse beating in her throat as the semi's diesel engine blended with the sounds of the night. She gave Denise an extra second to leave, was mildly surprised when she didn't, then stepped on the accelerator and sped down the road.

Pulling directly into the pathway of the

semi-tractor, she blocked its escape. There were three men in the high cab. Their menace flooded her system with adrenaline, making her realize how foolhardy she had acted. But someone from the sheriff's department should be here any minute, she told herself.

"Oh God," Denise exclaimed in a high voice.

"It's okay," Meg said, patting her on the leg. "Just hang in there."

They had locked the truck doors in the hopes of buying time. What had she been thinking, Nicky wondered, as the semi backed a few feet down the road in order to gain space to get around her. She put the truck in reverse to again block the tractor and trailer, but the semi was moving toward her, unable to pass freely, pushing the bed of her truck sideways as if it were a minor obstacle. "Fuck," she exclaimed.

That was when they heard the sirens. Nicky glanced at Meg, whose wide grin matched her own. Denise, pale with fear, smiled sickly.

"Hey, we did it," Meg said in the camaraderie of success. "I can see the headlines now: 'Women Rescue Cows.' "

Two deputies trained guns on the men in the truck, who grudgingly surrendered. They divided them between the squad cars, putting the two passengers in one and the driver in the other.

Nicky got out of her truck and examined it. Meg and Denise stood with her as she studied the tangle of metal that had been the bed. "Looks totaled to me. Now what do I drive to work tomorrow?"

"It might still be driveable," Denise said.

Dan and Natalie arrived late on the scene. The

police cars with their circling lights and chattering radios were still parked at angles in front of the semi-tractor trailer with its load of bawling cattle. Dan and Natalie got out of Dan's truck to stand among the gathering of neighbors and passersby. They looked bewildered.

"What the hell's going on?" Dan asked.

"These cattle yours?" one of the uniformed deputies inquired.

Sorting everything out in the dark took a couple hours. First they unloaded the stock, checked to make sure all the cattle were Dan's before turning them out onto pasture. Then they supplied the immediate information needed by the police.

When the sheriff's deputies drove off with the rustlers, leaving the emptied tractor-trailer rig marked for pickup by the side of the road, Dan and Natalie went to Nicky's farmhouse with the three women.

They sat around the kitchen table, congratulating one another. And Denise said with atypical timidity, "Do you suppose that's what happened to Brittle? Do you think he was kidnapped by rustlers?"

Looking with surprise at her ex-lover, Meg squeezed her shoulder. "I'll bet you're right." Her eyes softened as she smiled and explained to Dan and Natalie, "Denise jumped into the truck with us. She wouldn't let us go without her, would you?"

Feeling slightly nauseated, Nicky thought, she's going to forgive her. Ten to one, she'd even go back to her. "We better tell the police to check with Bill, the guy from the youth camp. Maybe he can identify the rustlers as the men who sold him Brittle for five-hundred bucks."

"Let's do that," Meg said.

"I almost forgot, we have news, too, though not as exciting as this." Natalie smiled at Dan. "I'm moving in with Dan."

"I thought you already had," Nicky said with a grin.

Nicky's parents showed up on Saturday, an unexpected visit. Her mother, deeply tanned and stylish in cotton slacks and sweater, stepped out of the Wagoneer as Nicky returned from a walk in the field with muck on her tennis shoes and dirt on her jeans. How was it that her mother always seemed to arrive when she looked her grubbiest, she wondered as she leaned forward to kiss her on the cheek.

"How are you, Nick?" her father boomed, grabbing his daughter in a robust hug.

"Good, Dad. You both look terrific? When did you get home?"

"Yesterday, dear." Her mother wrapped her arms around herself. "It's so cold here."

"I thought it was a nice day," she said, still disconcerted by their appearance and holding Scrappy at bay. She didn't want his dirty paw prints on her mother's beige pants. "But I suppose it must seem that way to you after Florida. Want to go in the house?"

"Yes. Where's Natalie?"

"I think she's cooking up a storm at the country club." Nicky glanced around the yard before going inside. It had that unkempt look that followed winter, after the snow melted and before the growing season began. "We had some excitement here last week."

"I heard something about that," her father remarked, patting her on the back as she opened the door. "You were a heroine. Nattie told us on the phone the other night."

Her mother noticed her surprise. "She didn't tell you we called, did she?"

"We only talk to each other in passing." Apparently Nattie hadn't told their parents that she was now waking up with Dan. She certainly wasn't going to be the one to break the news to them. Instead, she said before either of them could ask, "And yes, she's still seeing Dan."

"I know that, dear." Her mother sat at the kitchen table while Scrappy nosed her hand, looking for a pat. "How about some coffee?"

"Go lie down, Scrappy." Nicky poured the last of the morning's coffee into two cups and put them in the microwave. Then she made fresh.

"We're proud of you, Nick." Her father winked at her.

"But you shouldn't be so careless with your life, dear. You could have been shot."

"Or worse," Nicky added with a grin.

"Nicole, there's something I want to talk to you about before anything else." Her mother gave her an appraising look that kicked Nicky's heartbeat into high gear.

"Honey, can't it wait? We just got here."

She gave her husband an indecipherable look. "No, I want to get it out of the way while it's still fresh in my mind. Then we can get on with the more pleasant chitchat."

"I told her this is foolishness," her father said to Nicky, further alarming her. "I'm going outside."

Nicky set a cup of coffee before her mother and met her eyes. It was the look, the tone of voice, the insistence on clearing something up while it was "still fresh" in her mother's mind that set off her warning system. She took a deep breath.

"You know we play bridge with Mark Forrester's parents. They told us that Beth left him, that he's devastated."

Something akin to a hot flash raced through Nicky, bringing a flush to her face. She nodded in answer to her mother's raised eyebrows.

"They have a son, who stayed with his father, who needs his mother."

Nicky licked her lips nervously. She felt like a teenager again with a guilty secret and found herself unable to turn away from her mother's eyes.

"What I'm wondering is, did you have anything to do with her leaving her husband?"

"Mom, I don't mean to be impolite, but that's just none of your business." Her voice shook a little, betraying her worry at talking to her mother this way.

"I thought so. You and Beth were just too close."

She couldn't move or look away. Instead, she chewed on her lower lip and listened to the thudding of her heart, her body uncomfortably suffused with heat. There was no way she could explain her feelings for Beth, and she made no effort to defend herself.

"Is she going to move in with you? Can I ask that?"

Shaking her head, she replied, "No, not now anyway." A long pause followed, during which her discomfort reached the squirming level. "Mom, don't look at me that way."

"What way?" Her mother sighed. "You're my first-born."

"I don't need any more guilt."

"If you would like to see a counselor, your father and I will pay for it."

Maybe she should take the offer, Nicky thought, remembering her confusion over Meg and Beth. "It's not something you change even if you want to, Mom."

Her mother pressed her lips together, a sure sign of displeasure. "Okay. I tried," she said, dismissing the subject. "We'd like you and Natalie to come to dinner next Saturday night. The rest of the family will be there. We're cooking out."

Relief washed through her at being let off the hook so easily. But it left her feeling that her mother had only been confirming long-time suspicions. "Can we bring anything?"

"Just yourselves."

XVI

"You're going to what?" Nicky asked, looking up from the Sunday funnies.

"Denise wants me to go to counseling with her. I said I would." Meg shrugged. "What harm can it do?"

"I thought you had already split."

"Well, I'm not moving back in. We're just going to find out what went wrong." Meg leaned forward in her chair, her arms on her knees. She looked troubled.

"Why are you doing this? Do you like punishing yourself or what?"

Throwing the paper on the floor, Nicky leaned forward too. "I can tell you what went wrong. Denise wants to control you."

Meg studied her hands, her shoulders slumped. "I have to do this. I can't even tell you why. Maybe because I feel so guilty."

"Oh, for Christ's sake," Nicky exclaimed, getting to her feet and pacing the porch.

"I know, Nicky." Meg spoke softly. She got up and put a hand on Nicky's shoulder. "There's something between you and me. I'm not sure what, maybe just a spark. But you're not ready to give up Beth either."

Nicky felt stricken, her arguments shot down by the truth. "I *knew* you were going to give her another chance." It was going to be lonely if Meg moved out. "If you're not going back to Denise, will you continue to stay here?"

"Do you want me to?"

Would that be less painful? Nicky nodded. "Yes, I hope you will." Perhaps she would have some influence that way. Maybe she would be able to rescue her from what she considered a fate worse than death — living with Denise.

Meg visibly brightened. "It's time to start showing anyway. Will you still go with me?"

"Sure." Nicky was resigned. "Do you feel better now that you know Brittle was probably taken by those guys who tried to steal Dan's cattle?"

"I feel that he's pretty safe. They're not going to take him again, even if they don't end up being jailed very long. That would be too stupid." She added, "I'm glad it wasn't a horse person."

"So am I," Nicky agreed.

* * * * *

Comparing her present life to her circumstances last spring brought Nicky satisfaction. She had toughed it out, had made a niche for herself doing the work she enjoyed and at which she excelled — selling her prints through Margo, setting up a successful part-time business in Photo Perfect, even working at Photoplay. And now Margo was suggesting a one-woman exhibit of Nicky's photography.

Resting her elbow on the open windowsill, she ran her fingers through her wind-blown hair. What if no one came? What if none of her work sold? Agitated, she shifted her position on the truck seat and agonized over yet another worry.

Should she confront Beth with her suspicions or just ride them out? That was the question she needed to answer before she got home from work that afternoon. Beth was due back from New York, might even be at the house. She knew that if Beth was fooling around with Nancy Brown, she couldn't stop her. And she struggled nearly every waking moment to not think about the two of them in compromising positions. If she asked and Beth confirmed her hunch, she would have to do something. But if she did nothing and said nothing, would the end result be any different?

No cars were parked in front of the barn. Nicky breathed deeply with relief. She walked toward the house through warm sunshine, sensing that if she stood still long enough she would see the grass grow. The urge to plant was upon her. She longed to set out tomatoes, beans, squash, flowers, but knew if she did, they would surely freeze out.

As she freed Scrappy from the confines of the house and he threw himself against her legs in mindless adoration, Beth's Probe pulled up next to Nicky's truck. Absently, she patted the dog while she watched Beth get out of the car and remove her suitcase from the trunk.

"Here, let me help you with that," Nicky said, hurrying toward her.

Beth smiled in welcome. "Good to see you, sweetie. How about a hug?"

Taking Beth in her arms, she smelled her familiar odor — her particular cologne, the soap she used, the scent of her skin. Her warm, pliant softness comforted Nicky. Could she give this up? She held Beth at arm's length and looked into her hazel eyes, admired the high cheekbones, the trim figure. She longed to let down Beth's hair and run her fingers through it. Leaning forward, she kissed her lightly on the mouth.

"What is it, Nicky?" Beth asked, her smile turning hesitant.

You're cheating on me, that's what. She smiled crookedly and shrugged inwardly. Since she wasn't ready to let go of Beth, she would play what she called the pretend game. She would ask nothing, figuring the less she knew, the less it would hurt. "Tell me about the trip."

"Not much to tell, really. I went to meetings. I did eat some good meals, though." She put her free arm around Nicky and threw her head back. "What a glorious day to come home."

"I have to tell you about the cattle rustlers." She'd told Beth some of it over the phone.

"I want all the details."

Nicky gave them to her in bed. Hungering for Beth as she hadn't since she and Meg had succumbed to desire, she experienced a fierce possessiveness and wondered if it was rooted in fear. Reaching inside, she felt the moist walls tighten against her fingers. "I want you," she muttered between clenched teeth, meaning she wanted to establish territorial rights.

"You've got me," Beth said, catching her breath when Nicky, hovering over her, turned around to burrow between her legs and take her in her mouth.

Feeling Beth scoot under her and wrap her arms around her hips to pull her down, Nicky too gasped at the warm touch of tongue. Consumed by the hot river of desire flowing between them, she heard her own harsh breathing as she struggled to hold off climax. Then, shuddering with release and feeling Beth respond in kind, she collapsed face down on Beth.

Slowly, Nicky reversed her position to taste Beth's breasts, to embrace her and kiss her lips, her fingers still engulfed in passion. She smiled and sighed contentedly.

"Nice homecoming. I'll have to go away more often." Beth covered Nicky's dampness with a hand and leaned over her to gently take a nipple in her mouth. "So even Denise is a hero. And it looks like these rustlers took Brittle. Does that mean Meg is going to start showing him in earnest again?"

Nicky arched her back. "Yep. She's getting Brittle ready for this weekend." Why had she let Denise go with them on that harebrained attempt to stop the rustlers, thereby making her look good in Meg's eyes? "What I did was just a knee-jerk reaction. It wasn't heroic. Meg was my support. Denise was scared to death. She and Meg are going to counseling."

"Together?" Beth raised her head in obvious surprise.

"Yeah," Nicky said, feeling a stab of pain. What was it about Meg that she couldn't give up? "And on Saturday Natalie's going to tell our parents about her new living arrangements. Mom will be thrilled."

Beth rested her head on the pillow and studied Nicky's face. "You're just full of news. But I bet you're wrong about Cleo. She'll handle it with her usual aplomb."

"Think so, huh?" Then she confided her mother's questions regarding Beth's separation.

"And you told her to mind her own business? Nicky, you never cease to amaze me. I would have said that your mother intimidated you."

And you would have been right, she admitted silently, unwilling to give voice to it. "Wish you could go with me Saturday, be a part of the family."

"Well, I certainly couldn't do that after this revelation." Beth looked thoughtful. "Someday we'll go to family functions together, sweetie. Maybe we'll even instigate them when we're living together."

Nicky smiled and gave Beth a hug. At this moment she chose to believe her.